Stella Ryman and the Fairmount Manor Mysteries

"Stella Ryman no more entertained the idea of becoming an amateur sleuth than she had of entering next spring's Boston Marathon."

Mel Anastasiou is a writer and editor who divides her time between Bowen Island, BC and St Albans, UK. Her personal highlight was hearing her poetry performed by Dame Helen Mirren. She has not yet acquired Stella's life experience, but she keeps her deductive powers on overdrive to channel the strength and humour of the somewhat cranky sleuth. "Well," Stella retorts, "if you lived in Fairmount Manor, you'd be cranky, too."

By Mel Anastasiou

The Fairmount Manor Mystery series
starring octogenarian sleuth Mrs Stella Ryman in

The Stella Novellas
Spring 2014
   #1, Stella Ryman and the Fairmount Manor Mysteries (The Case of the Third Option and Stella vs the Dragon)
   #2, The Poison Pen Affair
Autumn 2015
   #3, The Four Digit Puzzle
   #4, The Case of the Vanishing Resident
   #5, Stella and the Thief Named Edge
   #6, Stella Ryman and the Man with the Gun
Winter 2015 to Spring 2016
   #7, The Death of a Crusader
   #8, The Ghost at the End of the Bed
   #9, The Mystery of the Mah-jongg Box

And in September 2015, **look for Frankie Ray to run off to Hollywood and get into more murderous trouble than you'd think a schoolmarm and hopeful extra could find in 1934.**

The Extra, A Monument Studios Mystery, Book 1

Stella Ryman and the Fairmount Manor Mysteries

Stella Novella #1

Mel Anastasiou

Copyright © 2014 Mel Anastasiou

Line drawings by the author

All rights reserved.

ISBN: 1517089441
ISBN-13: 978-1517089443

DEDICATION

With love to Maureen Docharty
and her mom
Velma Docharty

Without you I would never have met Stella.
With you, I learned about strength, smarts, and humour.

CONTENTS

1 *Stella Ryman and the Case of the Third Option*, Stella's introductory short mystery.   1

2 *Stella vs the Dragon.* A Fairmount Manor Mystery. Stella Novella #1   5

"Live or die, live or die! That's all anybody does around here. For once, I wish somebody would come up with a third option."
–Mad Cassandra Browning

STELLA RYMAN AND THE CASE OF THE THIRD OPTION

CHAPTER ONE

On this particular sun-and-shade April morning at Fairmount Manor, Stella Ryman no more entertained the idea of becoming an amateur sleuth than she had of entering next spring's Boston Marathon. For not only was Stella eighty-two years old, but she had lately sold her home and a lifetime of gathered possessions and washed up at Fairmount Manor Care Home in such a state that she would have bet her remaining seven pairs of socks that she'd be dead in half a year.

And here she lay in Palliative Care, only three months in.

At this time of morning, she reckoned that the rest of Fairmount Manor residents, in their ones, twos and threes, would be engaged with daytime television, or else sitting poised for the lunch tone to sound. But Stella was lying flat on her back and all alone, tucked up tight in a metal-framed bed in a shadowed upstairs room. Her fingers danced across her blanket, like little birds unsure where to light.

Of course, she was new at dying. A first-timer. Just like everybody.

She would not be afraid.

Soldier on, Stella.

She felt as if she were floating, and it took almost every scrap of Stella's concentration to make sure the sensation was taking her upwards. There should be no need to fear your own demise if you were ascending. Of course, if she felt like she was falling downwards, that would be quite another matter.

She bit her lower lip and attempted to trap one flapping hand with the other. In this way she managed to get both her hands folded across her breast. Her model for this posture was the Lady of Shalott, although at her age no Lancelot would be standing by to regret her passing. She tried to imagine Dr Terry—who looked, now she thought of it, something like Lancelot if the parfait knight had gelled his hair—sighing, "*She has a lovely face, God in his mercy lend her grace, Stella Ryman.*" Ah, well. To Dr Terry, as to the world, Stella was an old lady dying Upstairs in Fairmount Manor as best she might. Eyes firmly shut, she took a long slow breath.

Somebody slapped her in the face.

It was a light slap, but sharp for all that—sharp enough to hurt. It felt like the kind of slap you used to receive in the schoolyard as a child, when you'd royally teed somebody off—a bully, maybe, or one of those terrible, touchy friends you made from time to time throughout your life, the difficult ones who were so hard to shake.

"Wake up, Stella Ryman," a voice hissed from the side of the bed. "Stop this nonsense at once."

This specific halitosis was unmistakable. Stella's eyes snapped open. She looked up into Mad Cassandra Browning's furious, tearful face. At eighty-eight the woman was six years older than Stella herself, with grubby bare feet and a single streak of white in her mad Medusa hair. Cassandra's jacket was striped with bars of light and dark from the half-closed blinds in the window behind her, so that Stella was put in mind of a convict who has taken over the prison and is making demands.

Stella floated a little bit sideways.

"Damn it all," she muttered. Then it occurred to her that whether or not her early religious instruction had been in all ways accurate, she couldn't possibly exit this life swearing. "Blast!" she thought, and then, in an attempt to clear her slate: "Bless us every one." She tightened the clasp of her hands across her breast.

A drop of something wet hit her cheek. Unclasping her hands, she brushed it away. Another drop rolled down into the corner of her mouth. However, Stella wasn't the one who was weeping. Mad Cassandra's tears dripped down upon Stella's face.

Stella's heart softened. "It's sweet of you, Cassie, but please don't cry."

"I can't help it." Mad Cassandra's eyes shone damply in the shadowy room. "You're like an elephant."

Patiently Stella said, "I'm not like an elephant, Cassie."

"You're behaving exactly like the elephants in the National Geographic magazine, the ones that think they know when they're going to die and then they go away and do it."

Stella had read about elephants—The Elephant had been a favoured subject for children's written reports in the school library she used to administer—and she could easily picture the great beasts, with their dignity and poise, choosing their own moments to depart the earth and quietly slipping away. Considering the source, this was a lovely compliment, and she thanked Cassandra for it.

Mad Cassandra loomed above the bed, her tearstained face shadowed by her long hair. "Don't you thank me, missy. You've got no business acting like an elephant when you're needed downstairs. There's a problem."

"What problem?" Stella's interest flapped its ears for an instant. Then she remembered where she was and what she was meant to be doing. "I'm sorry, Cassandra, but whatever the problem is, I'm afraid I can't help. They had to wheel me up here on a gurney. I'm getting weaker with every moment."

Cassandra snapped, "That's because you haven't eaten in days. I heard that Reliza girl say so when she took a moment away from making eyes at young Doctor Terry." Dashing the tears from her furrowed cheeks, Cassandra stared fiercely round the little upstairs room until her face transformed itself with a ferocious grin. "I know what to do. Wait here. Or else!" With a final bang of bony fists on Stella's bed rail, Cassandra was gone from the bedside.

"Or else, what?" With relief—with disappointment—Stella closed her eyes once more. She shifted her legs and moved her clasped hands lower, down to her warm belly. No matter how she wriggled, she couldn't seem to rediscover her inner Lady Shalott.

As well, the room she had thought silent a few minutes before now filled with buzzes and blips from the machines outside in the corridor. The machines were as difficult to ignore as those dreadful people who always hummed the same songs. But above these ambient noises, Stella now heard a new sound—familiar and homey—that of the click of a key-pull opening a can. In the hushed little room there arose an aroma that recalled to Stella her days as a young mother. Baked beans.

Mad Cassandra breathed on her again. "Open your mouth, old woman."

"Old woman! Pot libeling kettle," Stella retorted, but she had to open her mouth to do so. A spoon slipped between her lips. She suddenly found her mouth full of cold baked beans.

"Now, swallow that directly."

"Not on your…" The second spoonful of beans followed the first. Fool me twice, shame on me, Stella thought. Just in time to avoid a third spoonful, she pressed her lips together. The tip of the spoon poked at her lips, between them, and then up against her teeth. It was so important to keep one's own teeth into old age, Stella thought triumphantly. This spoon shall not pass!

Then, quite clearly, as if in a film projected against the ceiling tiles above her bed, Stella remembered the day long ago when her little daughter Junie, wearing a new pink raincoat, had danced into the kitchen and declared herself starving for the bean soup Stella was stirring up on the stove. "I'm a little pink piggy," her daughter said, and they both laughed themselves breathless. It had been a moment of incomparable beauty. In fact, it was the memory best suited to the present occasion.

So, that was what had been missing: she needed a perfect final recollection before she died. And now she had it. Picturing Junie laughing around her spoonful of soup, Stella attempted to relax back into her previous position.

"You are the most irritating woman," Cassandra growled. "Listen, Stella, it's a well-known cure of the Ancient Romans. If you have a sick person, you feed them beans. Beans, beans, beans! Until the system slips back into whack and you're fit as a horse."

How historically interesting, if true, Stella thought.

"Feeding me is a waste of time, Cassie. You know why they've brought me upstairs."

Cassandra made a noise like that of a horse denied oats. "Live or die, live or die!" she complained. "That's all anyone does at Fairmount. For once, I wish somebody would come up with a third option."

"A third option?" Stella blinked. "How can there be a third option to life or death?"

But Mad Cassandra didn't answer. With a whispered curse, she stepped away from the bedside. Stella heard the sound of bare feet pattering away at speed.

She shook her head. Cassandra was certainly crazy, but she was agile as a forty-year-old. Perhaps it was some sort of trade-off for her loss of logic, like the way Stella was always losing her way to the dining room but could remember Who Did It in every Agatha Christie mystery she had ever read.

Stella was wiggling her badly placed pillow out from under her shoulder when she became aware of youthful steps in rubber-soled shoes. They crossed from the door to the bed. A moment later a gentle hand clasped Stella's.

The young care worker Reliza asked, "Are you perhaps feeling a little better now, Mrs Ryman?" With her other hand, Reliza pushed her shining dark hair back over her shoulder. Her lovely face flushed, and Stella knew that Reliza was about to mention the doctor. "I had to come when... somebody... Dr Terry!... told me that you'd been moved upstairs into Palliative Care...'

"How kind you are." Stella patted Reliza's hand. She cast about for something comforting to say to her young visitor. Cassandra's imagery lingered, oddly appealing in its use of personification and imagery, so

Stella added, "Sometimes I think we are all like elephants, finding our own time and place to leave life."

She'd meant to comfort Reliza. Instead, Stella had a sudden vision of herself trapped in a line of ancient and implacable elephants, waving and trumpeting their way through the long African grass on the way their dying grounds. Amid the crush and thunder of their feet, how could one possibly turn back?

> *I don't belong here. I'm not ready to be here.*
> *I've gotten myself into the wrong lineup completely!*

When Stella looked about her again, Reliza had slipped away.

Feeling nervier than ever, Stella wished that Cassandra would return. She yearned so fiercely for some kind of company now that she didn't care how irrational the woman was, with her mad talk of a mysterious Third Option to life and death. Here in Palliative Care, Stella's options seemed to be diminishing with every second. She wondered how it could be that people reported seeing their past lives flash before their eyes at moments like this, near the brink. Stella had no desire to reflect back on her childhood, her lightning marriage or her long career in the school system. She found herself thinking instead of feats she had never attempted, like para-sailing, and childhood dreams that had never come true—zookeeping, spying for the government, singing on radio, and above all these, becoming a detective… "I'm so sorry," she told the child she used to be. "I know you always wanted to become a clever detective and solve mysteries to the amazement of friends, family and the public at large. I never even tried, did I? But there was Junie to provide for. So, I hope, young Stella, you will forgive me."

All at once Stella became aware of feeling cold all over, nose to toes. She tried not to think what this sudden drop in temperature might mean. Trembling, she fumbled for the nurse call buzzer that hung by the side of the bed, but Cassandra had somehow tangled the cord so that the end with the button was jammed between the mattress and the bed rail. She freed it at last, and pressed it hard. Once, twice and three times.

Nobody came. She pressed the call button once more. And again.

There was no avoiding the question now. Was she dead? Had it had already happened?

And if she was dead, how would she know? Everything in the room looked much the same. The door to the corridor stood open at the same angle, just as Reliza had left it. Stella craned her neck to see whether the stripes of light on the floor had moved with the passage of time. She thought not. However, she noticed that the machines out in the corridor had fallen silent.

You heard so many reports of what happened when you died. The closer you got to the far end of life, the more of these stories you retained. Stella knew, of course, about the light you were meant to see. And that in the moments just after death there was reported to be brain activity, sometimes known as "the dream before dying". In that moment, you might believe you were alive when you were not.

Fooling herself was not good enough for Stella. She was one to weigh both sides of an issue. When teaching Science, Composition and Library Skills, problem solving, both inductive and deductive, had always served her, and Stella recognized that this might well be an outgrowth of her childhood desire to be a detective. Certainly, she saw no reason to stop employing her problem-solving methods now.

First, she identified the problem: If she was dead, how would she know it?

Stella wished she had a piece of paper, a sharpened pencil and a ruler, with which to draw a table. Squared-off graph paper would be best for the task. But, in the circumstances, she must do without. She was amazed—and somewhat disturbed—at the sleuth-like calm with which she logicked out the points that argued she was still alive:

1. She was conscious of her own rapid heartbeat.

2. The aroma of baked beans still hung in the air from Cassandra's visit.

3. She was a little bit hungry.

These suggested she was dead:

1. The sun did not appear to have moved since Reliza had left.

2. The machines outside the door remained silent.

3. She was growing chillier with every passing minute.

Stella struggled into a sitting position, groaning at the slow and painful articulation of her middle back. She pulled the skirt of her nightgown out from underneath her. She dangled both legs over the side of the bed.

With one hand on the small of her back and one on the bed rail, she managed to stand up. The floor rocked under her feet, as if she'd left the safety of land for the roll of a ship at sea. Conscious of her cold toes—cold feet, today of all days! How very apt!—she wiggled into her blue terry slippers. As she did so, she knocked over Cassandra's empty can of beans. The can fell sideways half under the bed, rattled and lay still.

Light through the open door to from the corridor drew a bright runner across the pale tiles of the floor. It was the same sort of illuminated carpet the moon rolled out before you on the water. When she was a child, Stella had been certain that if you could just master the trick of it, you might walk along that golden pathway towards a distant shore.

But by now, it was midday. There was no moonlight. But in front of her on the floor was the shining pathway of light from the corridor, and there was the door to the corridor. Or… the Door.

Which?

Stella slid one slippered foot forward. As her foot caught the light, she was astonished to find that she had unconsciously solved *The Case of the Third Option*. The answer to Mad Cassandra's puzzle came to her quite suddenly, and so clearly, that she chided herself for not seeing it sooner.

Of course! How simple, if you thought it through. For Death was undeniably a mystery, but any fool could solve it by dying. And Life was so thick with questions that answering one only served to raise a dozen others.

But there was, after all, a Third Option.

The Third Option had not been there all along, yet it was here now, spread out before her in the fan of light from the open door.

She stood up a little straighter. To take the Third Option, she must not know what was outside that door. More—it could not matter whether that door opened into an Afterlife—or Nothingness—or back into the cabbage-y, pine-scented corridors of Fairmount Manor Care Home.

For the Third Option was Adventure.

Of course, nobody would be saved if she passed through this door. She must not hope to win true love or find her fortune. The act of adventure would only be added to the list of unknown deeds of pure and useless courage that formed the dreamy blue unconscious of busy humankind.

Was it possible not to care whether you were alive or dead? For walking through that door must be an act of pure enterprise.

Stella shivered. No epic hero facing unasked-for adventure could have felt more reluctant than Stella did at this moment.

Stella edged the toes of her blue terry slippers right up to the margin of the carpet of light leading out of the little room. Yet she could not summon the nerve to move them even one inch further. Looking about her, she spied the empty can of beans on the floor where it had rolled. Stella shuffled back towards the bed and picked up the can of beans and the spoon. She looked around for a trash bin, but couldn't see one, and anyway, what would she do with the spoon that was rattling inside it? She couldn't throw that in the bin. It was a perfectly good spoon, licked clean by Cassandra's tongue.

As Stella stood undecided, holding the can and the spoon, the door opened wider in a draft from somewhere out of her line of vision. To Stella, the movement signalled impatience.

And now the door caught a draft from another direction. The opening began to narrow. She sensed that her opportunity was closing with it. Folding her lips in the determined manner of the career school librarian, Stella leaned the empty can against her pillow, with the spoon inside it sitting up in bed like a tiny, round-faced patient.

Soldier on, Stella.

Without further thought, Stella slipped out through the door. It closed behind her. Her open-heeled slippers made a snicking sound as she hurried past open rooms into which she dared not glance.

CHAPTER TWO

Stella reached the door at the top of the stairs before she was struck by the smell of pine cleanser.

Was she alive, then? The odour of pine, strong as peppermint, cheered and reassured her. Heaven—or Hell, for that matter—might echo life, or even be echoed by life, but it would certainly not smell of pine cleanser. So, for what it was worth, Stella was still among the living residents here at Fairmount Manor.

An hour before, Stella had believed herself past all expectation of even a brief new chapter in the book of Stella Ryman. But now, she had solved the *Case of the Third Option*. And she had taken up adventure when it called.

Now she drew a long breath, arms outstretched, so that her nightgown brushed her knees as it rose. Her chest expanded with a heroic wellbeing. Then she remembered that, beyond her earlier idea of dying, she had made no other plans for the day.

Ahead of her, she recognized the rhythm and slap of bare footsteps disappearing down the corridor towards the stairway. She heard a ghostly voice. No...

She heard Cassandra Browning's voice: "Stella

Ryman, somebody's crying. Did you forget what I said? You're needed downstairs."

Of course, Cassandra was crazy. But for Stella, who had experienced no demands upon her time for the three months since she'd arrived at Fairmount Manor, the words were like the horns of a distant company of questing knights.

After it, follow it, follow The Gleam...
She followed Mad Cassandra.

STELLA VS THE DRAGON

Stella Novella #1

CHAPTER ONE

Stella stumbled around a corner, one hand on the wall for balance. Now that she had followed Cassandra downstairs, she couldn't see the infuriating woman anywhere. Blinking, and only just managing to stay upright on her slippered feet, she did her best to take stock of the corridor before her.

On her right, the door read: Room 33. Stella's heart rose. What color was the sponge pattern on the corridor?

Yellow. That meant she was in Daffodil Corridor. And, when she turned to her left, she was facing Room 34. Her own room. She had left it only that morning when Cheryl, the care worker with the Giaconda smile, had wheeled Stella upstairs to die.

Well, she was back. And although nobody could call Room 34 palatial, it was her home. Had been so for the last three months. Inside Room 34 her own bed would be awaiting her—a single bed of reasonably generous proportions, with an excellent mattress from Sears. It had been her final indulgence before coming to the care home, and worth the breathtaking price tag.

Grateful for home and bed, Stella was more than ready to lie down again.

But then she saw it: the suitcase on the floor outside Room 34. Stella had never seen this suitcase before.

It sat.

Outside her room.

All black, like an anvil.

She shuffled up close of to the suitcase. She didn't have to employ her deductive mind to predict that it would be heavy with somebody else's worldly goods. This suitcase and its usurping owner loomed between her and the only place left in the world where she could lay her head. Fairmount Manor had given her room to somebody else.

Her insides swam, and she identified the feeling as one she had last experienced several decades before, when as a middle-aged woman she had opened the door to her younger lover's rooms. There on his mat, with the toes pointing towards his bedroom, had stood a pair of shiny red kitten-heeled sandals that were not hers. Those bright sandals had lit up the doorway, bright as a lipsticked smile meant for somebody else. She'd closed the door and turned away, because the red shoes had stood for heartbreak.

She couldn't turn away now. This black suitcase outside the door to her room meant something even worse. Something more basic even than love. So, alone in Daffodil Corridor in her open-heeled terrycloth slippers and nightgown, Stella tried to think how to fight for her home. But somehow her slippers pulled her away from Room 34, urging and tugging her down along the corridor towards the stairs. And she might have kept going, all the way back upstairs to Palliative Care, had it not been for

the open Staffroom door and what she saw inside it.
    Something lay on the floor that shouldn't be there.

CHAPTER TWO

Look at that.

If there was anything that proved that Fairmount Manor existed outside the great teeming world of ordinary people, it was the sight of a woman's handbag lying with its guts spread out across the floor. Anywhere else in the real world, the handbag would have been on its owner's shoulder, or tucked away in a locker or the bottom drawer of a filing cabinet. But here among the elderly, the bag had been left out on a shelf just inside the Staffroom door, whence it had fallen to the floor.

Stella touched the handbag with the toe of her terry slipper.

Residents were meant to stay out of the Staff room. But how could she leave a fallen handbag as it was? Cheryl, the care worker with the Mona Lisa smile, would soon notice the mess and clean it up. But the younger, the loving Reliza, would walk right by—not because she was lazy, but because her head was sure to be in the clouds after Dr Terry's last visit. Being in love made Reliza even kinder than she used to be, but no better at all at housekeeping.

Steadying herself with a hand on the shelves, Stella bent her knees deeply. They made an ominous sound as she shifted her weight. You know you're old when you bend down to tie your laces and look around to see if there's anything else you can do while you're down there. She had once thought that joke funny.

Stella let go the shelves and sat down with a thud on the cold floor, one bare leg bent to each side of the mess of papers and coins that had fallen out of the handbag. She then remembered the old advertisement: I've fallen and I can't get up. The ad had been meant seriously, but had inspired a cultural wave of satirical chuckling at the elderly. How glad she was now that she'd never found that particular ad amusing. Grimacing, she pushed her glasses into place and set to tidying the handbag's contents back inside, leaving the letters until last. The coins slipped around a bit, but she got most of them and with her fingers swept a few pennies that would never be missed under the shelves to the right of the door. The letters were much easier to deal with. She packed them neatly together and sighed over the message repeated on each one, with what appeared to be increasing emphasis. She was not a nosy person—really she wasn't interested enough in other people's letters to be nosy— but she was a reader, and as long as her vision was behaving itself she couldn't help reading anything put before her. On each page the letters were large and the warnings ominous.

"…your payment in arrears…"
"…call our department immediately…"
"…you have not responded to messages…"

Feeling like a sneak, Stella slid the letters into the handbag and shut it. Then, having first heaved the bag up onto the counter, she got slowly to her feet. She held onto the counter, breathing heavily and staring at the handbag in front of her.

It looked all wrong sitting out in plain view, as if somebody could just take it.

Stella took it.

She hung the bag over her arm. How naked she used to feel without her own handbag. It had been a brown shoulder bag she'd carried for years, never needing to change it. She'd bought it in Mexico, charmed by the intricate leather punching in the shape of leaves and grasses. For the first year, everything she put into it came out smelling a little like a burro.

Enjoying the everyday weight of the handbag on her arm, she took a step out into the corridor. There, she paused to consider where a person deprived of her room might go for help. But as she wavered in the empty corridor, a quiet but compelling sound reached distracted her from her worries. She turned back towards Room 34—her room by rights—now the room of the suitcased stranger. Certain now of what she was hearing, she took a couple of steps nearer the door. A couple more…

There was no mistaking the sound of a woman crying.

Somebody's crying, Stella Ryman. So, Cassandra had spoken truly.

Yet many residents must cry from time to time. In fact, although she remembered little from her first days at Fairmount Manor, Stella did recall sobbing herself to sleep her first few nights here. But what surprised her about this particular sound of crying was the timbre of the voice—there was no rasp of age to it. The woman who was crying was young, far too young to be a resident of Fairmount Manor. Ridiculously too young to be moving into Room 34.

Stella cocked her head towards the sound of the sobbing young woman.

And on the day she thought she'd die, something inside her—something sharp of eye and mind—stretched and turned with a swirl of a great tweed cape. Stella smelled wet wool, the fog off Baker Street, and pipe tobacco.

As she moved towards the door, she murmured, "Here's a mystery."

CHAPTER THREE

Due to safety precautions, residents' doors at Fairmount Manor were never locked. Stella had never managed to resign herself to the lack of privacy, but just now it made things simple. She slid the handbag back just above her wrist where a handbag belonged. Then she opened the door to Room 34.

There on Stella's stripped-down Sears mattress, a yellow-haired woman sat weeping into a tissue as if her last hope had gone.

Stella took a step inside the room. She had thought to find a stranger in her room, not a member of Fairmount Manor's staff. "Cheryl?"

Holding the tissue to her nose, Cheryl looked up. "Mrs Ryman! Are you better, then? I tried to tell the Director not to make us move you upstairs…I'm so happy to see you." Tears overtook her again.

It would break your heart to see Cheryl so tender and pink around the nose and eyes. She appeared drawn, and older than her thirty-something years. What could so upset Stella's favourite care worker, Cheryl of the Giaconda smile?

Stella made her way to the visitor's chair near the bed and sat down. She set the handbag on the floor beside her and asked, "Cheryl, has something happened to one of your children?"

Cheryl shook her head.

"Well, then things can't be so bad…?"

"It's so horrible," Cheryl burst out. "They say I stole something."

"Nonsense." Stella darted a sidelong, guilty glance down at the handbag she'd taken.

"That they would even think such a thing…" Her tears returned, in greater volume.

"You're as honest as the day is long. The Director must have a copy of your personnel file in her office, and that's your documentation." Stella, having worked in the teaching profession for forty years, had extensive experience in cheering up crying women. Whether they were teachers or parents, she could calm them down in moments, given access to tea. Here in Fairmount Manor, and without any tea to hand, she was happy to see that the knack had not left her. As she spoke, there was a visible receding of the tide of tears, and a lightening of the area under Cheryl's eyes. Briskly, Stella took the next step. She asked, "Now, who are they? I mean, who said such a terrible thing about you?"

Cheryl said, "It was Mrs MacAndrew, across the hall. You know."

"Of course." The lie came automatically—just now Stella hadn't the slightest idea who lived across the hall. But a moment's reflection while Cheryl dabbed at her eyes with a tissue brought recall.

Mrs Alice MacAndrew. Stella folded her arms across the front of her nightgown. "I call her the Dragon."

Cheryl nodded, and Stella could see that she was trying to smile. The care worker sat up and pulled another tissue out of the sleeve of her pale blue smock. As she blew her nose, the teddies on her smock danced a little. It occurred to Stella that she had never seen Cheryl wear a different uniform. She must wash it every night, Stella guessed, because it was invariably clean, and pale blue showed the dirt like nobody's business. Stella was reminded that the care worker was the main support of her three small children. And wasn't there something dodgy about the husband? But she couldn't think what. How appalling, not to remember what this nice woman had confided in her.

"Everything will be all right. I'm sure it will…"

"I can't see how," Cheryl said.

Stella realized that this was one of those conversations into which she was doomed to interject banal phrases such as this one. Yet, to counter cruel acts, you really needed phrases that were broad in scope and as easily recognisable as a friend's face. "It will all work out, you'll see. Tell me, what does the Dragon think you stole?"

Cheryl straightened herself and let out a long, tired-sounding sigh. "A coin."

"A coin?" Stella frowned. "That seems very small beans to me, Cheryl. How would rich old Mrs MacAndrew know whether she had one coin more or less in her possession?" Privately, Stella considered that this accusation sounded just the cuckoo sort of resident complaint that the staff members at Fairmount Manor were expected diplomatically to ignore.

But Cheryl was shaking her head. "This was a valuable coin. An antique…'

"…and worth quite a lot of money," Stella

clarified.

"Yes."

"I see." With a nod to Robert Browning, Stella thought: Somebody gave orders. All smiles stopped. There were harsher acts than unfounded accusations, she knew, but such indictments were quite cruel enough.

It occurred to her that an obvious and important question needed to be asked. She looked down at the handbag beside her. Ah, yes. "Why you, Cheryl? Not that any of the staff appear to me dishonest, but why you in particular?"

"That's exactly what's so awful." Cheryl pulled at the hem of her teddy bear patterned smock. "Mrs MacAndrew is such an unreasonable woman, and she never comes out of her room because she's afraid somebody will steal her things…'

Stella nodded. "I've heard she brought some real treasures with her…"

The care worker continued, "Mrs MacAndrew won't leave her room, so she has her meals brought in to her. And she doesn't want Ollie or Reliza, because—you know."

"Because Mrs MacAndrew is a racist old so-and-so," Stella finished for her.

"Yes. Well, to be fair, some older people did grow up that way." Cheryl's blue-grey gaze entreated understanding. "Of course I don't agree with it. But anyway, she liked me. She requested me, and I went because she seems so frail, and because the Director asked me to. I had to spend less time with people like you, people I like, in order to help Mrs MacAndrew out. Mrs Warren—the Director—made it sound like a compliment."

Institutional management. Stella snorted. "And so,

when the coin went missing...?"

"Mrs MacAndrew said it was me who took it. It could only be me. Because I was always in there. Because I tidied and dusted her things for her. And because…'

There followed a short pause, while the word because hung in the air. Stella found herself gazing down at Cheryl's handbag again. With care for her joints, she reached down and hoisted it into her lap.

She said, "Because you need the money more than most."

The silence between them was heavy with agreement. Stella lowered her head. Reluctantly, she held the handbag out to Cheryl. "I think you must have set this on the counter in the Staffroom. I found it spilled out on the floor into the corridor. I'm afraid that when I was tidying everything back inside, I happened to see the letters from the credit card companies. I'm very sorry."

Cheryl reached out for her bag and Stella let go of it, rather the way you relinquish a baby to its mother. Thanking her, Cheryl opened it and looked inside, as if to check whether anything was missing. This was not a tactful gesture, but it was so natural and automatic that Stella couldn't take it personally.

Stella said, "The Director will realize that the Dragon is simply a foolish old woman spouting nonsense." She nodded sharply. Take it from a foolish old woman who knows. "That coin will turn up somewhere silly, like in the toe of her slipper, or down the side of the mattress nearest the wall." She pictured the Dragon, pawing and clawing over her treasures inside her wealth-packed Room 33. Stella gazed around her own Room 34, empty of everything but chair, bed, dresser and the only picture Stella had brought with her, hanging over the dresser, of white ducks in a shadowed pond, stone cottage under a British-blue sky.

Cheryl, holding her bag tight against the front of her smock, sat up straight, as if facing an accuser. "Mrs MacAndrew said I took the coin when she was in the washroom. She's in the washroom a lot."

Stella nodded. She spent a certain amount of time there herself.

Cheryl continued, "The Director herself, Mrs Warren, searched the room from top to bottom, even though you know how many expensive knick-knacks and bits of furniture she's got. Mrs Warren couldn't find it."

The Director herself had searched the room… Stella floundered, trying to think of something that would help. She'd already said that Mrs MacAndrew was an old fool. She supposed that this might bear repeating. But somehow, without willing it, her eye came to rest on the picture that was hanging over the dresser. They must have left it hanging here, for the new resident. Somebody ought to have asked permission, she thought. It was almost the only long-term possession she'd brought from home. Undeniably it was a poor copy of an obscure and sentimental landscape, and she couldn't remember now why, out of all the bits of art she'd purchased from time to time over seventy years, she had hung onto this one. She must have chosen it. Wrapped it. Packed it. She tried to remember bringing it here, but could not. Yet she clearly remembered the list of items she'd ordered from catalogues, beginning with her excellent mattress.

"…but we've all had police checks," Cheryl was saying.

"Yes?" Stella knew she sounded vague. She did her best to refocus on the conversation.

The care worker sat up a little straighter, balling her tissue in her fist. Her pallor had returned. "But anyway, thank you for listening, Mrs Ryman."

"Right." Stella shook herself. "What can I do to help? Shall I go and see the Director? I will testify to my complete faith in your honesty and integrity…"

But the crescents beneath Cheryl's eyes had deepened to a delicate lilac. "Thanks, but there's nothing…"

She didn't finish her sentence.

Silently, Stella finished it for her: There was nothing the elderly Stella could do. She was simply too old to be of help.

Stella frowned. How wrong Cheryl was. Stella would see the Director. She would make herself heard. Stella had once been an effective advocate for school library funds and staffing. She was just the person to help this poor woman to keep her job. And then, by jingo, she would get her room back. They could move the stranger with the black suitcase elsewhere.

At the sound of a rap at the door, both women turned.

Ollie's familiar form filled the doorway. He was carrying something in one hand.

The large care worker's gaze travelled from Stella to his colleague Cheryl, and he hefted a black suitcase from one hand to the other. "Something wrong, Cheryl?"

Shaking her head, Cheryl blew her nose into another tissue.

Stella could not take her eyes off the black suitcase in Ollie's hand. The stranger's suitcase… no, the usurper's suitcase.

She would not leave Room 34! They would have to pick her up and carry her out. Which Ollie was perfectly capable of doing, should such an action be required of him.

Stella's throat felt thick and sore. Soldier on, Stella. She would not cry. "Please don't bring that suitcase in here."

Following her gaze, Ollie looked down at the suitcase he held in one huge hand. "I was told to take this upstairs for you, Stella. You're feeling better, though, I see. Have you come back down for a visit?"

"I beg your pardon?" Stella looked again from Ollie to the suitcase. Yes, it was the black one, the same stranger's suitcase that had been sitting outside the door of her room.

"Your suitcase, Stella." Ollie held it up.

"My suitcase?" Ollie was wrong. "Mine is brown leather. My mother gave it to me, long ago."

Politely Cheryl asked, "Might you have bought a new one before coming to Fairmount Manor?"

Stella cursed the tremble in her voice. "If it's mine—is it? With my things in it? —then please just leave it here inside my room."

She did not like the look Ollie and Cheryl exchanged. Then she recognized the problem they would have with her request: institutional management again. Firmly Stella said, "I've come downstairs. I won't go back to Palliative Care."

"But the paperwork…" Cheryl began. "It's not that easy once you…'

Ollie interrupted cheerfully, "Mrs Warren gave the paperwork to me. I've already done it. Can't be undone."

Stella sat down on the bed. "I don't want to go back up there," she said to Cheryl, the woman she had just offered to help. How preposterous Stella's dreams of standing up to the Director now seemed. "I can't. It would be the end of me. Cheryl, please help me."

Before Cheryl could answer, Ollie laughed. "It's

God's Waiting Room up those stairs, all right. Now, Stella, I tell you what. Paperwork can't be undone, but it can be ripped up. As if it never happened. Doesn't hurt me, and it's good for you."

Stella caught one hand in the other before her and clasped them to her middle. She had never warmed to Ollie—it was nothing to do with his size or ethnicity, of course, but more with his laugh. There were certain laughs that rubbed her the wrong way, and she saw now that this too was a sort of prejudice, and she was sorry for it.

She thanked him. He set the suitcase in the middle of her floor and said, "Welcome back home to Room 34, Stella my bella."

"Thanks, Ollie." Still feeling shaky, she smiled up at him. "You're very…jolly."

He laughed and left, as Cheryl climbed down off the bed and opened the suitcase. The lid fell back onto the floor. Her own pastel leisure suits—bought expressly for Fairmount living—along with her nightclothes and other familiar garments, lay neatly folded inside.

"Would you mind setting my case on the bed, please?" Stella asked. She hadn't known her own suitcase when she saw it. Cheryl had been quite right to reject Stella's offer of help—an elderly woman with nothing but leisure time made a wonderful listener.

And nothing more.

"I'd like to unpack myself, and find something to wear…"

"I'll help you dress, Mrs Ryman," Cheryl said. She blinked hard, appearing at last to pull herself back together. "You've had a hard day."

The offer was welcome, and resonated with warmth. I'll help you dress. Stella remembered dressing her little daughter Junie all those years back, the care and love she'd put into folding down her daughter's cotton socks, buttoning her strawberry-coloured cardigan up the front. And the sad day that came at last when Junie had firmly said, I can get dressed myself, now, Mother. It had been enough to break Stella's heart.

"Thank you, Cheryl," she said firmly, "but I can dress myself."

Once the door had closed behind the care worker, Stella stood for a moment, feeling exactly the old fool she was. Then, with hands that were still none too steady, she began to struggle out of the nightgown in which she'd expected to die.

CHAPTER FOUR

The click of her door and a hiss in her ear woke Stella from a miserable night's dreaming that Cheryl was weeping behind bars. But as she struggled back to consciousness she identified the sibilant voice as that of Mad Cassandra Browning: "Stella Ryman! I was right, wasn't I? You're back among the living."

Stella groaned. The grey light between the window blinds above the bed told her it couldn't be more than five in the morning. Did Cassandra, at eighty-eight, not understand how difficult it was in old age to get a reasonable night's sleep? Once awakened, Stella's window of opportunity for falling back to sleep narrowed with every year on this earth. She shouldered her way deep under the covers and gave a soft but penetrating false snore.

Footsteps padded away from the bed towards the door. And then past the door and into the washroom. Cassandra was taking a little tour of the premises.

Keeping quite still, Stella breathed into her trusted sleep mnemonic. *A, my name is Allison, my husband's name is Arthur. We come from Abbotsford and we sell…*

But Cassandra returned. "Stella! I'm sorry I abandoned you upstairs. I want to show you something wonderful, to make up for it."

Cassandra's whisper tickled Stella's ear.

"...*we sell artichokes.*" There was no telling how Cassandra would define the word wonderful. Stella soldiered silently onward with her mnemonic. The bed heaved as Cassandra climbed up onto it. Stella clutched at her sliding duvet. If either of them had been any fatter, they would certainly have fallen off with it. Cassandra bounced the bed a bit, and, as usual, Stella envied the older woman her agility, although not that stringy, witch-like hair. "B, my name is Bridget…"

The sheet snapped back and light touched Stella's eyelids.

"Stella! Do you want to meet some dead people?"

"Oh, Cassandra. No thank you, dear." Stella sighed. She struggled to sit upright. Her cotton nightgown—a different one from the nightgown she'd worn upstairs—caught her under the arms. "If you tell me your room number, I'll come visit you when I do get up," she promised. "I can't recall your corridor—is it Primrose, Chrysanthemum, Daisy…?"

Cassandra clasped her hands against her narrow chest. "Please, just let me do this for you, Stella…?"

Cassandra leaned closer, her gaze too bright and her breath too terrible to bear. She took hold of Stella's hands and pulled. Yet even Mad Cassandra could not easily raise Stella so early in the morning. Not without straightening out her various limbs… But, for a miracle, as Cassandra with her wild and wiry strength hauled her out of bed and upright, Stella's hips did their job with hardly a complaint.

Standing before the bed, in her stretch velvet

tracksuit and grubby bare feet, Cassandra's eyes grew wide and pleading.

Letting go again, she vanished through the door.

Stella didn't mean to follow. She meant to turn right into her own little washroom, where the water was warm as a younger lover's kiss. But although she might have resisted the pleading in Cassandra's eyes, those bare feet with their cracked heels and horny yellow toenails filled her with such sorrow that instead she set her glasses on her nose, pulled open the door to the corridor and followed Cassandra through.

Out in the empty, low-lit corridor, Stella looked to her right. That way was a dead-end, with nothing but a fire door leading to the outdoors. So she made two fists and padded left along the corridor, past closed doors with their family photos and drawings by well-loved family members of the elders within. "Whatever makes us happy," she thought bitterly, with a backward gaze at her own undecorated door. As she came around the corner into the empty Corridor Park, she saw Cassandra just ahead. Feeling the full weight of an unwanted friendship, she followed the woman round the corner.

Cassandra looked back at her over her shoulder, a delighted frown on her face, and then led Stella down a short corridor that smelled of cold steam and bleach. Stella hadn't thought about laundry since she'd left her own house. Now, somebody did it for her. Who? She hadn't thought to ask who was drying her sheets and rolling her underwear into neat little nylon sausages. Perhaps she was old fashioned—of course she was old-fashioned—but she hoped it wasn't Ollie.

Cassandra stopped at the end of the corridor. Stella stopped, too. She shifted her weight from one hip to another, to loosen her midsection a little more. As she did so she read the little black signs on the two doors to the right. Both doors were labeled Staff Only, and she resisted an almost unbearable urge to open them and walk inside. Across from these doors, against the opposing wall, stood a large faux-wood cabinet, half blocking the single door on that side of the corridor.

Cassandra slapped the cabinet. "Sometimes this wheelie cabinet blocks the door. The room in behind the cabinet is like *Brigadoon*—you can only find the way inside on certain magical days." She nodded at the door beside it. "Today, we can get in. You do want to see the dead people, don't you, Stella?" she asked again.

"Oh, Cassandra." Stella wished to heaven the woman could have been just two inches saner.

Cassandra arched her brows winningly. "They're very sweet."

Stella crossed to read the label on the door. Printed in white letters against black laminate, it was difficult to make the word out, even with her glasses on. Her vision swam, as it sometimes did, but there was only one word, and that not a long word. It read, Effects. Stella wondered what this could mean… Special Effects. Sound Effects…Cause and Effects…

The door would be locked of course, and Stella said so out loud. Cassandra nodded and covered her laugh with the palm of her hand.

Stella tried the handle. It turned. The door opened. Very curious now, she led the way through. Touching the wall to left of the door and then to the right, she found a light switch and flipped it.

Before her stretched a long narrow closet. It was shelved from floor to ceiling in cubbies of the same golden-red, highly grained wood that she associated with school closets built in the 1950s and 60s. Each shelf was jammed with articles. Before she could see what they might be, Cassandra pushed past her and wandered down the aisle space between the shelves. She danced her fingers from shelf to shelf, and then paused, beaming, about halfway to the far wall.

"I know you," Mad Cassandra said to the cubby. She reached inside and pulled out a length of cloth—purple velvet. A gold fringe on the ends fell across Cassandra's prominent knuckles. She greeted the scarf with obvious pleasure. "Why, Joy Hammaguchi, as I live and breathe!"

Understanding blossomed in Stella. The purple velvet scarf was one of the unclaimed effects of dead residents. "Cassandra, are these the dead people you wanted me to see?"

"These are all that's left of them. The possessions that went unclaimed when they died." Cassandra wrapped the late Joy Hammaguchi's scarf around her neck and smoothed the fringe across her bony breast.

"Their personal effects…" Stella shivered, as much on account of the company as the morning's chill on her bare arms. She looked down and saw that she was still dressed only in her nightgown. Again!

Cassandra slipped round behind her and set herself in front of the door to the corridor. The shelves stuffed with the belongings of past—very much past—residents of Fairmount Manor rose to either side of her like the steep walls of an ancient, treasure-filled tomb.

"I should go back," she told Cassandra.

"But isn't it nice here?"

"Yes," Stella lied, although she did like the feeling of quiet and privacy she felt in the narrow cubby-lined space.

"Don't you feel as if you are among friends?"

"For Pete's sake, Cassandra, stop trying to scare the dickens out of me." Stella wandered a little way towards the far end of the narrow space, where a window admitted green-filtered light. She ran her fingers across the spines of several books. One fell over in its cover. Reaching from behind, Cassandra snatched the book up and pressed it into Stella's hands. "This is for you," she said breathlessly. "To make up for leaving you Upstairs."

"That's very nice of you, dear," Stella said. Never before had Cassandra sustained contrition for any length of time. Remorse didn't suit her at all, and yet the gesture was touching in its way. Stella stared down at the worn red-covered edition of *The Prisoner of Zenda* that Cassandra presented to her. A nice bit of storytelling, that one, despite the *Bridges of Madison County* ending. Opening it at random, she drew in the velvety old-book smell. She looked down and read,

"If we go back and tell the trick we played, what would you give for our lives?'

"'Just what they're worth,' I said..."

Just what our lives are worth. In her own case, exactly what would that be?

Stella said, "Thank you. But I must go back now, Cassie."

"Why?" Cassandra asked. She didn't stay to be answered, but slipped out through the door, closing it behind her with a heavy click.

Heart thudding, Stella hurried to the door. She pulled at the handle. It would not open.

CHAPTER FIVE

At first, Stella thought she must be mistaken. Doors had a tendency to seem to be locked, but then opened at a second attempt. She wiped both palms on the skirt of her nightgown and tried again.

The doorknob would not turn. She called out, and then banged on the door with her fist and the flat of her hand. Then she fell silent and listened, but heard no response.

Butterflies of unease began making a fuss inside her chest. She tried not to imagine a cleaner wheeling the cupboard outside across the door to the Effects Closet, obscuring it from searching eyes. This cupboard was indeed *Brigadoon*! It might easily vanish from sight, never to reappear for a number of years. Or anyway, not until it was too late for Stella.

She took a step towards the window, but, as so often happened, panic blurred her vision and spun her balance out of whack, so that she stumbled against a shelf and had to use both hands to regain her equilibrium.

Clumsy! Exactly when had all that yoga she did in her sixties worn off? Shaking her head, she made her way down towards the window. As she tugged on the cord to raise the blinds, she made grand Prisoner of Zenda-like plans for opening the window and escaping through it. But once the blind was up, she could see that it was the sort of window that did not open. Moreover, outside it was nothing but laurel hedge, grown thickly up against the glass, so she could not even gesticulate for help.

She sat down on the carton beneath the window and rested her feet on an expensive-looking leather-bound photograph album that might have been left on the floor for the purpose. Disappointment overtook her.

Nobody, even at breakfast, would miss her—she'd missed breakfast too often to worry anyone on that account. However, by lunch, Cheryl or Reliza might notice that she was not to be found in her usual chair beneath the skylight in Corridor Park. And Ollie! Yes. That made three to search for her. Three to come to her rescue. They would not look in this closet first, but they would look in it eventually.

But what did she mean by eventually? And would anybody even remember to look inside the Effects Closet? There were so very many doors and rooms in Fairmount Manor. And, as she sat on her carton, staring at the door, it occurred to her that the Effects Closet doorknob was unusual, and possibly unique in the building. All the doors she'd ever seen in Fairmount Manor had a latch—a lever—that you pushed down on to open. This one had a knob that was meant to be turned, most likely an anachronism left over after an institutional remodel.

That meant this particular door was rarely used. It might very easily be overlooked in any search. Stella might never be found at all.

"I should never have followed Cassandra," Stella said aloud. "It was a very foolish thing to do. I should have turned on my heel and headed back home to Room 34."

Yet the blame was not solely down to her. Management had a stake in this, too. Imagine! Having a cupboard in a care home that locked automatically and could not be opened from within. It was a very silly state of affairs. Very poor management... unless the truth was that Cassandra, in a fit of puckish madness, had deliberately locked Stella in here.

She breathed in, right down to her diaphragm, the way she'd learned in those yoga classes she'd taken so long ago. Then she exhaled up through her collarbone, throat and nose. She tried to remember exactly what Cassandra had said before she left Stella alone in the cupboard. She thought it had been the single word Why? But why had Cassie asked Why? As she inhaled again, the answer came to her.

Cassandra had wanted to know what Stella had to do that was so very important that she couldn't spend a little time with the dead people in the Effects Closet. Well, Stella knew the answer to that one. She had to:

-eat her breakfast. (But she wasn't even hungry).

-make her bed. (But one of the care workers would do it for her).

The truth was, nobody needed Stella. The only person counting on Stella to get out of this closet was Stella herself.

A sort of hmphing sound emerged from the back of her throat. She glared at the door. How she would like to have the chance to ask Cassandra, "Well, Cassie, what's so all-fired important about your morning? Got to spread some of that patented craziness around? Lock some more old ladies into closets?"

She leaned back against the cool glass of the

window and stared between her feet at the photograph album beneath them. It was an expensive bit of work—green snake skin, or something that looked very much like it. Her left foot half covered the name printed in gold on the front cover. *MacAn*....

She moved her foot and read, *MacAndrew*.

What was Mrs MacAndrew's photograph album doing among the Effects of the dead? Alice MacAndrew, the Dragon, was very much alive, so much so that it was she that had accused Cheryl of theft.

Stella remembered now how Cheryl had wept.

And, with shame, what Cheryl had told her: There's nothing you can do, Mrs Ryman.

One after the other, Stella kicked her heels against the carton. They made a hollow sound, like the thumps that began plays at the *Académie Française*. Thump. Thump. Thump. And the curtain rises... The detective enters the scene.

After all, if she ever got out of this cupboard, there must be something that she could do for Cheryl.

With one toe she opened the cover of the photographic album. Mrs MacAndrew, many years younger but still recognizable by her Dragon's glare, stared up at her.

Stella glared back.

Letting the album cover fall shut, she stood and walked to the door. With a sense of energy she'd not thought to feel again, she pounded her fist against it. Again she called out several times. And when at last hope failed, she rested her forehead against the door and whispered, "Damn you, Cassandra."

In the moment of quiet that followed, she heard what she was sure was the sound of quiet laughter. She tried the knob again. It turned, and the door opened.

She was halfway through before she remembered to snatch up The Prisoner of Zenda. Clutching the book to the breast of her nightgown, she made her escape.

CHAPTER SIX

Washed, dressed, and on her way back from breakfast in the dining room, Stella was trying so hard to think of a way to approach the Dragon that she nearly knocked over a woman from Fern Corridor. Without a glance for Stella, the woman stabilized her walker and doggedly clicked on by.

Once she'd steadied herself, Stella made her way towards Daffodil Corridor. She passed the yellow trolley standing alone, the one that Ollie was always leaving here and there while he disappeared for twenty minutes at a time. She suspected that he smoked, although that was none of her business. Well, bearding Mrs Alice MacAndrew was none of Stella's business, either. As she raised her hand to knock on the Dragon's door, she found this an unexpectedly cheering thought.

Into the belly of the Dragon. Stella squared her shoulders. Be calm. Be rational. Tame her with reason.

She waited. Then, having received no reply to her first knock, Stella rapped again, a little harder. No one answered, but no one said Go away, either. Taking this as an invitation, she let herself into Mrs MacAndrew's room.

Once inside, she was prepared for wealth and bad temper. Even more, she had imagined a certain Miss Havisham gloom. But she had never thought to find, in the eleven by fifteen-foot space allotted to each of the residents of Fairmount Manor, such shining and cheerful abundance.

In the course of her long and often over-full life, Stella had known the interiors of countless rooms arranged by women whose tastes ranged from miniature ornamentality, as Stella liked to call the condition, to ponderous elegance. Mrs MacAndrew's smallish room out-ornamented and out-eleganted them all. The bed was cherry wood, and the bedside table ebony, inlaid with ivory. Crystal bowls, tole vases and more clocks than even busy people needed snuggled together atop every gleaming, lemon-scented table and étagère. Under Stella's feet a red Turkish carpet overlapped a white wool Chinese carpet overgrown with flowering vines. All around the room, the walls were chequered with large and small paintings hung in Mondrian-like patterns, frame abutting frame and—on the wall holding pastel portraits—jowl rubbing up to jowl. A vanity table, richly bobbled, was stacked with leather bound albums of varying dimensions—of which one must be missing, Stella thought, remembering the album she'd found in the Effects Closet. But would the Dragon even know it was gone, amid such a plethora of luxe? The room reminded Stella of her last visit to London, twenty years before.

"It's like walking into Woolworth's…" she said aloud. "…and finding yourself in the British Museum."

Behind her, the washroom door clicked open. "Isn't it just?"

Mrs MacAndrew, smelling strongly of hyacinth soap, stalked past Stella and clambered up onto her bed.

Stella attempted to aid her in the climb, but for her trouble was gifted with a Dragon's glare. Mrs MacAndrew pulled an embroidered throw blanket across the lap of her velveteen lounging suit.

"I heard you were dead," Mrs MacAndrew said. There was no way to know whether she was criticizing the accuracy of her source or Stella herself for disproving the rumour.

So, the woman was going to be even more difficult than she had imagined. Stella cleared her throat. Dragons or no Dragons, the world sent too few opportunities for an apt quotation to let one go by. "The report of my death was exaggerated," she said.

"Misquotation!" Mrs MacAndrew straightened a tapestry bolster at her back. "Mark Twain. Such an easy one to get right, too."

Stella had not got it wrong, but in the face of all this polished and lemon-oiled splendour, her mother's good manners kicked in and she did not correct the woman.

"Well, Stella? You barge in here and disturb my morning…" While the Dragon spoke, several clocks about the room struck the hour. Stella counted an ormolu, a glass-domed Victorian model and a lavishly carved Swiss monstrosity over near the velvet-draped window. But it was the clamour of the mahogany Grandfather near the washroom door that Stella recognized, for its deep toll had often awakened her in the small hours, when fatigue and boredom diminish hope.

The Dragon finished, "…so, what do you want?"

"I'll sit down, shall I?" The overladen vanity had a small matching stool. Stella pulled it up beside the bed and sat down.

"How's the weather outside? Spring-like, I

suppose?"

"I'm not here to talk about the weather," Stella said firmly. "I'm here to save you from making a fool of yourself."

Mrs MacAndrew sat up a little straighter. "You can save yourself the trouble. I'm no fool, Stella Ryman. And I don't have to explain myself to you."

This was absolutely true.

"Even so, accusing a member of staff of stealing a coin in an over-furnished…" Yes, she would say it. She waved a hand to encompass the objets d'art, the cheek-by-jowl furnishings, and the paintings quilting the wall. Half the ceiling blossomed forth with prism rainbows from the crystal bobs on at least five lamps. "…in an over-furnished traffic jam like this, is very foolish indeed."

Unladylike, Alice MacAndrew snorted. "I see you have no eye for art," she replied. "These are objects of great beauty…'

"…and joys forever. Very shiny, too." Stella yielded the point. Then she pounced. "Polish them yourself?"

The Dragon's eye flamed in Stella's direction. "Cheryl helped. As you well know. I also had help looking for my family's missing coin when it went missing. I am not an unreasonable woman."

Stella asked, "Is it reasonable to threaten a staff member over a single little coin, especially when you have so much? I call that crazy, Alice MacAndrew, and I won't be the only one who thinks so."

"That coin," Mrs MacAndrew said, "has been in my family for many years."

It was Stella's turn to snort. "I used to keep a sock full of pennies in my kitchen drawer."

. "The stolen coin was privately minted not long after the Battle of Culloden, in 1745. It had a picture of

Bonnie Prince Charlie on one side, and Flora MacDonald's bonnet on the other. The MacAndrews married into the MacDonalds, you know." Alice MacAndrew proved that her face held at least one smile. Stella had a momentary vision of the woman as she must have been like as a small pugnacious child on the playground.

Stella reminded herself of her vow to keep calm and rational, no matter what the woman said. "You don't say," she murmured.

"I do say," The Dragon countered, clearly enjoying herself now "Furthermore, some years ago, the Bonnie Prince Charlie coin was valued at fifteen thousand dollars. It would be worth more now, wouldn't you say?"

"I suppose so." Stella scanned the room, attempting to guess the number of places, shadowed and narrow, that a coin might have rolled under or into in this forest of valuables. Just thinking about such a search was fatiguing.

Stella said, "Well, I'm going to find that coin, and then you're going to feel like a very silly woman."

Mrs MacAndrew descended—from the bed to the floor, and also from haughtiness to the vernacular of the schoolyard.

"Takes one to know one," she said. "Where are you planning to start, anyhow?"

"Where did you keep the thing in the first place? Not in your wash bag or underwear drawer, I take it." Stella rose from the vanity stool, one hand on a stack of albums atop the vanity.

"You've got your hand on it," Mrs MacAndrew said sweetly. "It's the top album, with the red crocodile binding. That's where my family keeps the coins from the Eighteenth Century." She turned with grace and made her way back into the washroom, shutting the door behind her.

Having made a rude face at the washroom door, Stella flipped open the cover of the album. She flipped through. It was one of those elderly albums with pages of thick, pungent grey cardboard. The pages were doubled, and coins of various sizes had been fitted into holes in each page. Most of the eight or ten holes on each page were full, and what must have been their provenances were listed beneath each coin in a spidery, illegible hand. Page after page of coins! It was all very dull stuff. Stella decided that she felt about coin collections the way she felt about butterfly collections—coins and butterflies were better off circulating naturally out in the world. The only collection of this sort she'd ever viewed with interest was her daughter Junie's Beatles bubblegum card collection. The full face of Ringo Starr had been lovingly framed in tinfoil on the first page. Flipping through the Dragon's album, Stella became more and more certain that nobody could love these coins the way Junie had loved Ringo Starr.

"What page was the coin on?" Stella called. "The Bonnie Prince Charlie one you're missing?"

"You mean, the coin Cheryl took," came the answer through the washroom door. "Eighteen."

Page eighteen was third from last in the volume. This page was indeed special—it held only one circle, about an inch in diameter. The circle was empty. An unreadable scrawl underneath, presumably offering an historical commentary on the coin, squiggled on down half the page. Stella studied the front of the cardboard page, and then looked at the back. It was indeed so like the pages of the album where her daughter Junie used to keep her Beatles cards… she remembered Junie's sobs when the picture of the Mop-tops fleeing the barber's chair went missing. Stella had eventually found it…

Aha.

At the top of the page, she pulled the two pieces of cardboard apart. She reached down inside, buckling the page somewhat. Then she shook the album. Something was in there, all right. With an effort, she turned the album on its side and a coin the size of a quarter rolled out. Stella found herself peering down at a stamped-out profile of the reportedly dissolute—but certainly Bonnie—Prince Charlie.

"There!" Stella said, as Mrs MacAndrew opened the door to the washroom. "Hold out your hand."

The Dragon did, and Stella placed the coin inside it. She continued, "You could have found it yourself, Alice MacAndrew, and saved everybody a lot of trouble. What would a person like Cheryl do with a rare coin, anyway? Surely that sort of thing is very traceable by the police, not like regular money."

Mrs MacAndrew cradled the coin in her palm, her thin fingers curling around it. Frowning, she examined one side and then the other. "I'm very happy to have this back. Where did you find it?"

Stella indicated the open album. "In between the two sides of the cardboard page. It had fallen through."

"I trust you will say nothing about the money in between those pages," Mrs MacAndrew said. "I hold you to your honor."

Stella stared. It seemed to her that the woman was talking nonsense. "What money? More coins?" There had been nothing else in the space between the pages.

"The thousand dollar bill," Mrs MacAndrew said.

Stella looked from the album to Mrs MacAndrew. "There was no thousand dollar bill in this book. Are you sure you're not doing that thing I do," she asked diplomatically, or fairly diplomatically, "when you mix up the decades and get the present time wrong?"

"Stella Ryman, are you gaga or just a poor listener? Pay attention! If there's no thousand dollar bill in there, then Cheryl took that."

"For crying out loud..." Well and truly infuriated, Stella turned back to the album.

While Alice MacAndrew barked exhortations to take care, Stella tugged the cardboard pages open at the top and looked between them, while coins fell out of their holes and clattered onto the vanity surface. Deep between the sides of the last page of the album, she spotted a bit of pink paper. She wiggled her hand in and caught the note between forefinger and middle finger. Somehow she pulled it free and held it up.

"I've never seen a thousand dollar bill before," Stella said. "I didn't know that the denomination was pink." It looked a little like Monopoly money, but the paper felt heavy and smooth between her fingers.

"It's Canadian legal tender," the Dragon said swiftly.

"I see." Pushing her glasses up on her nose, Stella peered at the bill and made a young Queen Elizabeth's face on the one side, and a monochrome landscape on the other. She held the bill out to the Dragon. "So here it is, and now you can call Cheryl in and apologize and make everything right." And, Stella decided, she herself was going to have a nice long lie-down before lunch. She felt as knackered as an old grey mare.

Mrs MacAndrew took the money from her and held it in the same hand as the Bonny Prince Charlie coin. She said, "That's all very well, but where are the others?"

"What others?" There were no more bills between

those pages.

"There was a thousand dollar bill inside each of those pages. Eighteen in that book alone. That makes…"

"Eighteen thousand dollars." Stella took a step away from the crocodile-skin album, as if it still had its teeth and would bite.

CHAPTER SEVEN

With this turn of events, any further argument in Cheryl's defence must be well thought-out.

Stella stared at Mrs MacAndrew. That earflap hair and dewlap mouth—or maybe it was her bright brown eyes—gave her an air of guard-doggery, but also of intelligent intransigence.

So, not just well thought-out. Any argument in Cheryl's defence had better be a humdinger. For example, posit that Cheryl needed money. This raised a question of logic: if she still needed money, then would it follow that she hadn't stolen any?

No. People who had money wanted more of it. Look at billionaires, all of whom wanted more money—even more feverishly, it seemed, than the poor. She was sorry to see her own logic fail, but returned to the centre of the argument.

Cheryl was honest.

Now, Stella knew what every schoolteacher knows: a true heart shines. But how, in the face of so much missing money, was she to convince Mrs MacAndrew of that? Stella decided that, heading into fierce winds in an argument, sometimes you needed—not force—but a different tack.

"This honest woman…" Stella ignored the guttural noise Mrs MacAndrew emitted. She repeated, "…this honest woman is a mother. Cheryl is the support of her children. With your accusations, you're endangering them and their home."

"Cheryl's children are her own responsibility. This is mine." Mrs MacAndrew held out her arms to encompass her trove of furniture, paintings, glass and clockwork.

Dragonish paranoia! "Nobody says they're not yours…" Stella began.

But Mrs MacAndrew interrupted. "No. You aren't listening, Stella. I mean that these are my responsibility. I safeguard these possessions for my family."

Stella said, "You only have a granddaughter."

"Bellamy will carry on after me." Mrs MacAndrew smoothed the silk coverlet with both palms. "My aunt did so before me, and her father before her. And his father… The chain of responsibility is unbroken. Would you have me break it?"

"No." Stella valued tradition, even though the idea of all those generations of fire-breathing MacAndrews was fairly daunting. "Still, these treasures are only… things. Objects, no matter how lovely. I'm talking about people," she said calmly.

"So am I," Mrs MacAndrews answered, just as evenly. "These beautiful things are the legacy of masters, the vision of the artist's eye. With help, they'll endure the centuries. But a painting can't protect itself against ill treatment, nor can a table flee the teeth of a family dog. Precious objects can't armour themselves against theft, either. That is up to me. I was raised to it—to know my duty to Chippendale, to Stubbs…" She gestured towards a pair of chairs near the window, and a small portrait in oils of a gentleman on horseback. "…and I owe it to those who had the foresight to collect and cherish them: the MacAndrew family. If I let a thief steal from me, why not open the doors to the nation's great museums and let burglars walk away with it all?"

Stella had managed so far to keep her mouth shut. Now she rose to her feet. "Alice MacAndrew, what a lot of nonsense. These are expensive chairs and paintings. Don't make it sound as if this room holds the last remaining works of Leonardo da Vinci. Nobody gives a darn about your Chippendale chairs except you and your granddaughter. And she'll probably sell the lot when you're gone. And there won't be a thing you can do about it."

Well, I guess you could haunt her, Stella thought, feeling a little breathless. However, when she took in the other woman's pallor she wondered whether she might possibly have gone a little too far. Mrs MacAndrew looked about two steps from the abyss.

"I'm sorry," Stella said. "I lost my temper."

The Dragon smiled faintly. "Your apology is not accepted."

Stella leaned forward. "Be angry with me, Alice. But not with Cheryl. She's the one who polished all this, isn't she? She's the one who dusted, who moved things about, and wound the clocks…"

At this moment, a cuckoo went off. Stella glared at the relic of old Switzerland. However, it had awakened in her the realization that her argument was sliding dangerously off target.

Before she could broach the question of the timing of the theft, Mrs MacAndrew said, "Well, Cheryl didn't clean and polish out of the goodness of her heart. I paid her. Extra."

Stella started. "What do you mean, you paid her? Fairmount Manor pays her."

"Now you see." The Dragon folded her claws across her lap. "I am a fair woman. I gave her one of those…" she pointed to the album. "A solid thousand dollars. She took it, mind you, with hardly a thank you. And then, I suppose, she must have seen where the money was kept, between the pages."

Stella stared. "Alice, there are only two possibilities here. One—that you believe, mistakenly, that you are telling the truth. And two, that you are lying through your teeth. No care worker in the world would be allowed to accept money like that." She stood up.

"Believe what you like," Mrs MacAndrew said. "I paid for her service. I'm no slave driver, and Cheryl worked hard. She took the money for it. Then she stole the rest. Please leave."

"With pleasure," Stella said bitterly. As she exited the Dragon's lair, she tried to slam it behind her, but the pneumatic door inhibitor wouldn't allow it. As it cushioned itself shut, one of the clocks went off again.

Stella wandered down the corridor in a stew, wondering just what Mrs Alice MacAndrew, with all that money, was doing in this place anyway. Why wasn't she in Montague House, with its chandeliers and wainscoting? Now, there was a mystery. But by the time Stella had passed through Corridor Park, where today Thelma Hu sat alone, she'd avoided Thelma's thrusting cane and deduced the solution to the mystery of what a very rich woman was doing at Fairmount. The answer was right there in the coin album: Alice MacAndrew had come to Fairmount Manor just because she had money. She thought she could buy herself excellence in service.

As she drifted into the foyer and up to the locked front door, she added to herself, and so that she could be the richest of us all.

But Stella could forgive Alice MacAndrew that. Everybody needed to feel as special as she could manage to be.

Crossing the foyer, Stella stopped at the window next to the glass door. She was not allowed to go any further—Stella was not allowed outside by herself—but from here she could look out under the awning and the visitor's drop off area. Leading up to the front door, the driveway curved up from the street. It had been edged with daffodils, and the way things were going, she was glad to have something cheery and yellow to look at. Even these late daffodils were better than nothing, although they wouldn't last much longer. Their ragged petals and trumpets bobbed in the damp-looking, grey spring wind.

Some of the daffodil stalks, Stella saw with a shock, had been clipped back. Clipped back! What kind of a gardener committed a crime like that? Not another blossom would they see from those bulbs, next year. The world really was not the place it once was. Daffodils were cut back, honest care workers were accused of crimes they would never in a million years commit…

As she fumed, a car turned into the drive, running over one of the daffodils and leaving it crooked and broken on the blacktop. As the SUV pulled up, she eyed its shining, expensive lines. Somebody's relatives were well to do, that was certain, although it was not a MacAndrew—The Dragon's granddaughter Bellamy was a struggling student, no matter what her inheritance would someday be. But this car! Nothing that big and shiny came cheap. It was German, she guessed. Further, she predicted that the driver would prove to be a young lawyer, or perhaps a dentist. But somebody in his twenties or thirties. Middle-aged men always seemed to own classic cars, or convertibles, didn't they?

She was pleased with her detective work when she saw the handsome youngish man climb out of the driver's seat and open the back door of the car. He was a very attractive fellow, the sort who would have turned her head back when, if she'd passed him on the street.

What she'd expected to see next, she didn't know. But she wasn't ready for Cheryl to get out of the back seat of this expensive vehicle. Cheryl, who until recently had driven a battered old compact into the ground, and after that had arrived by bus. Now she leaned inside the shiny German shark of a car, embraced her two children—Stella could just make them out—and then her handsome husband. He hopped back into the car.

Cheryl adjusted her handbag on her shoulder and walked towards the front door.

CHAPTER EIGHT

To Stella, watching the care worker's approach from the other side of the glass front door, Cheryl appeared to droop to one side. She seemed dragged down as much by the weight of her handbag as by fatigue or distress.

What she would do when Cheryl reached her, Stella couldn't say. For how might she ask for an explanation for this sudden show of wealth, the acquisition of an expensive car? Of course, Stella could invoke the elderly person's right to extreme nosiness, but the idea repelled her. Furthermore, if she did ask where the money to buy that shiny new car had come from, she dreaded hearing Cheryl's answer. For Cheryl was honest—and Cheryl would have to lie.

So, before the care worker could open the door, Stella turned and walked away.

As she reached the corner that would take her past the office (or possibly to the dining room—it was always so hard to know which corridor led where), Reliza and Ollie passed her, one coming from the left and one from the right. They greeted Stella—briefly—and headed straight for Cheryl as the foyer door shut behind her.

Stella stopped. She turned.

She watched as Cheryl looked from Reliza to Ollie. A moment of silence ensued, and then the handbag slipped off her shoulder and slumped on the floor at Cheryl's feet.

In a thin voice Cheryl said, "I can't tell my family about Mrs. MacAndrew's accusations. My husband Riley's only just come back to us. I must not upset the boat. But to have to defend myself alone…"

Reliza put her arms around the taller woman. "Especially when the Director believes they are true, and that you stole," she agreed. "But Dr Terry has told me he disagrees. And I do not believe you stole anything, Cheryl. Neither does Ollie. Do you, Ollie?"

Ollie, his broad face relaxed, was gazing out at the driveway where the big new car had just dropped Cheryl. After a short pause he said, "Of course not. Say, that's some car you've got…"

Cheryl rubbed at her eyes. "My husband Riley got us a new low interest credit card to ease the pressure. He worked it all out on paper. He said it'll save us money to lease a new car."

As she listened nearby, shame heated Stella's cheeks. She ought to have known better. She should have trusted her intuition. Cheryl was not dishonest—she merely had a spendthrift husband and an unclear grasp of personal finances. Thank God!

Stella took a step closer to the little triangle of care workers as Cheryl went on, "Riley says it's cheaper… It's sure nice for the kids…"

Unexpectedly, Stella found herself meeting Cheryl's gaze.

Taking a step forward, Stella clasped her hands together. She said, "Cheryl, I found that coin for Mrs

MacAndrew—the Bonny Prince Charlie coin."

"Oh, Mrs Ryman!" Cheryl's face lit with relief. She smiled her beautiful smile. Just for that one moment, the world was a brighter place.

Stella wished that she did not have to extinguish Cheryl's smile with what must be said next—the news about the missing eighteen thousand. But maybe she didn't have to. Perhaps, if she saved the bad news for later, Cheryl would benefit from a little break from stress and tears.

But holding such knowledge secret was a kind of a lie. And if Cheryl was to brace herself to meet further charges, Stella could not leave the news unbroken. She said, "There's going to be a second, worse accusation, Cheryl, and you must prepare to defend yourself against the new lie that will be told."

Reliza let out a small, wordless cry. Ollie turned away from the window and folded his strong arms across his chest. "What now?" he asked. "Are they saying Cheryl held up a liquor store? Robbed the National Mint?"

Nobody laughed. Reliza came as close as she ever could to hissing: "What, Mrs Ryman? What have you learned?"

Cheryl stood still. Her hands were clasped tightly together. Her handbag still lay on its side at her feet.

Stella said, "Mrs MacAndrew believes that she gave you a thousand dollar gratuity… and that you accepted it." She decided not to mention the thousands of other dollars that were missing. Yet.

Cheryl stared. Reliza and Ollie exchanged looks. Reliza's first language was not English, and in her agitation she stumbled over her words. "A thousand dollar tip?"

"That old woman is gaga," was Ollie's

pronouncement. "Loco rococo."

Cheryl was shaking her head, and looked as if she was trying to smile, of all things. "But I did," she said.

In the moment of silence that followed, Stella stood frozen with disbelief.

Apparently unaware of her co-workers' stares, Cheryl fumbled in her pockets, which were on the bulgy side. At last she pulled out a tissue and blew her nose. "Sure, I took it," she said. "Even with Mrs MacAndrew, I have to be polite."

"But we're not allowed," Reliza burst out. "Taking money from a resident can result in uneven care—Mrs Warren was very firm about that when she hired me. You could be fired for that." Her face had gone ashy.

"Only if they find out," Ollie interjected.

But Cheryl was waving her hands in a gesture of denial. "I took it, but only because I didn't want to hurt her feelings. Whatever she thought she was giving me, it's worthless. I've still got that so-called money she gave me."

So-called money? Stella struggled to keep up with what Cheryl was saying.

Again Cheryl delved into her pockets. She said, "It's in here somewhere. It's got to be." She bent down and fumbled in her bag. "When I work at the mall every December, to make extra Christmas money for the kids' presents, there's a list of currency that we're not allowed to accept. This one's on it. Thousand dollar bills have been out of circulation for ages. Decades. It's out of date. You can't spend it. It's just paper, like…" She turned to Ollie. "… just like Monopoly money. It's worthless."

"Worthless." Stella breathed the word. Relief ran through her like a cold drink of water in sunshine. "I should have realized." She wondered suddenly about Mrs MacAndrew and her treasures. Was that really a Stubbs hanging on the wall? What if the chairs were Chippendale reproductions, faithfully polished but without any true value? And what if the Bonnie Prince Charlie coin was a greater Pretender even than the original?

"Thank God," Reliza whispered. "You can't be fired for taking a bit of paper."

Cheryl began to weep, but it was a completely different sort of crying than it had been the day before in Stella's room. Stella felt rather like crying, herself, and Reliza, she judged, was not far behind.

Ollie raised one eyebrow. He cleared his throat. "Sorry, girls." With his look he included Stella among the "girls". "Money is money. Even if it's out of circulation, it's worth what it says. You can't spend it at a store, but take it to the bank, and a thousand is what they have to give you. A thousand smackeroos. Then, I guess, they shred the old bill, or put it in a museum, or something."

Cheryl had stopped crying. She had turned white and was holding onto Reliza, who appeared shaken to her centre. Stella looked around her, saw the visitors' chair near the front door and sat herself down in it.

"I don't know what to do," Cheryl said. She blinked. "Yes, I do. I have to give it back."

"No!" Reliza cried.

"Don't!" Ollie barked. He looked as serious as Stella had ever seen him. "It'll only get you deeper into trouble."

Reliza nodded. She took Cheryl's hands in hers. "You will certainly be fired, and maybe even arrested for taking it."

The care workers appeared to have forgotten all about Stella, sitting on the visitors' chair nearby. It was as if she'd disappeared, or become a ghostly presence. She could listen without having to speak, and see without being seen. It was a great relief to step away from all this tension and become invisible.

Ollie laughed without humour. "Arrested, no. Fired, yes. But they can't prove it if they can't prove you took the thousand. You know what you have to do. Get rid of it."

Still digging through her pockets for the money, Cheryl shook her head.

Stella wanted to say, Listen to them, Cheryl. But she did not. Leaving the situation to the young folk, she remained in her chair, invisible.

"A few years back," Ollie was saying, "at another home, this old fellow died and his brother gave me his car. A "95 Corolla. I just made up a story that it was my uncle's and drove it for a year, until the insurance ran out. No skin off anybody's nose. It wasn't a problem."

But Cheryl appeared to have stopped listening. "Could I have dropped that darn money? I couldn't, could I?" She picked up her handbag and was searching inside it as she walked away. Ollie and Reliza followed in her wake.

Left alone in sudden silence, Stella leaned back in the visitors' chair. She wished she didn't know what Cheryl would do, but of course she did. The woman couldn't behave any way but honestly, and nobody could stop her. Not Ollie, not Reliza, and certainly not Stella.

A stripe of sunlight had crept through the glass front door to lie across her slip-on shoes, like a small warm cat. She sat throughout a series of steady heartbeats within her own breast, enjoying the moment outside time, a moment of comfort wherein nothing at all was required of her. Then with a sigh she got to her feet and followed the three care workers. She reached Daffodil Corridor without losing her way—for once!—in time to see that Cheryl, still wearing her coat, was just entering the

Staffroom. Reliza and Ollie must have broken away for other duties.

Stella waited outside the Staffroom door. Although, she supposed loitering was the precise word for what she was doing. Loitering with intent.

She peeked through the gap between the door and its frame to see Cheryl weeping and sifting through her handbag again. As with so many things, it came down to luck. Would Cheryl find the money in her untidy bag and pockets right away? That would spoil Stella's plan entirely. Or would Cheryl blow her nose and wash her face before dumping everything out on the table?

Stella heard the washroom door close.

CHAPTER NINE

As she entered the Staffroom, Stella lifted her feet in her slip-on shoes a little higher than usual so as not to make a sound. Certain that the money was not in Cheryl's handbag—she'd seen its complete contents spilled out on the floor yesterday—Stella walked to the coat rack.

A few moments earlier, Cheryl hadn't been able to find the thousand-dollar bill in her coat pocket, but then Cheryl had been crying. Feeling cool and smooth as lemon custard, Stella dug into the pockets of Cheryl's blue coat. She fished out several tissues, even more shopping receipts, and the bit of pink paper that was worth, as Ollie had put it, a thousand smackeroos.

With the thousand dollar bill wrapped in her tightly closed fist, Stella hurried out, past the sink, which made her feel quite thirsty. There was no time, however, to stop to take a drink, not even a dash of tap water. She longed more than anything for a nice cup of tea, but the important thing was to remain unseen as she her escape. But before she'd taken two steps outside the Staffroom, she heard a murmur of voices: Reliza and Ollie were approaching. Stella's Room 34 was just an unlucky few yards too far distant to reach before they saw her. The money still in her fist, Stella ducked out of the corridor into the largish storage room just across from the Staffroom. Back to the wall, and quite giddy with secrecy, she listened to the conversation going on just across the corridor from her hiding spot.

"I can't find it… that thousand dollar bill is missing," Cheryl was saying.

Reliza answered, "That is the universe telling you not to get into any more trouble."

"I can't take the accusations much longer," Cheryl said. "I won't."

On the opposite side of the corridor, behind the door, scowling at the table beneath the storage room window, Stella sent an urgent mental telegram: Cheryl, hold on. Don't do anything you'll regret.

Out in the corridor, she heard Ollie say, "Be cool, Cheryl. This will all blow over. Mrs Mac's not the first person to lose something in a care home…"

As she listened inside the storage room, Stella held tightly to the money and gazed at the empty boxes stacked beside and on top of the wooden table. This table was the sort that high schools provided for art classrooms. If it had been a folding table, the articulated legs would have made it useless to her. But it had four straight legs at the corners and a green plastic tablecloth draped awkwardly across it.

With a start, she noticed that the hallway had grown silent. Cheryl, Reliza and Ollie must have headed off on their various duties. Her back still pressed against the wall of the storage room, Stella was alone in this part of the corridor.

It was then, with the money hot in her pocket, that the full import of what she had done crept up upon her like a thief. It snatched away her equilibrium and then her concentration. And then it left her staring blankly at the storage room table with its concealing green cloth.

CHAPTER TEN

Inside Stella's head, a dust storm of vagueness had overtaken her. Only one clear thought remained: she wanted a cup of tea. So, she strolled out of the storage room, across the corridor and into the Staffroom. There she looked about her, taking in the cabinets and the plastic chairs about the laminate table, where half a muffin sat among its crumbs on a paper napkin. This Staffroom was new to her, but really all school Staffrooms were much alike.

There would be tea in the cupboard over the sink. What kind of tea exactly you never knew—it might be berry tea, or even the devil ginseng. If she was lucky, she'd find orange pekoe. She pulled open both doors above the sink.

There on the second shelf a pot-bellied kettle trailed its long cord among a scattering of blue paper sweetener packets. A motley crew of mugs stood about on the shelf above the kettle, and on the right side of it sat an unnaturally large box of Red Rose tea. Lately, she'd been on an Earl Grey kick, but Red Rose would do. Would do very nicely, in fact.

It was a business to get the kettle down from its shelf. With its trailing cord it seemed to be part cat and knocked several packets of sweetener into the sink. Don't hurry yourself, Stella told herself. And not too much water in the kettle. You're not heating water for a bath, her mother added sotto voce in Stella's ear.

She plugged in the kettle and stood leaning against the sink, hands in her pockets to warm her fingers, which often felt a little cold.

There was a bit of paper in her pocket. It felt like paper money. How nice to find a bit of unexpected cash in her pocket! Perhaps this would be enough money for milk and butter to be picked up after work, on her drive home from school. Inside her pocket, she folded the bit of money between her fingers and watched the kettle. One of the mysteries of the beverage-drinking world was that the more you wanted a cup of tea, the longer a kettle took to boil. Kettles were indeed like cats—you had to act as if you didn't care what they did. Turning her back on it, she wandered over to the staff fridge, which was stocked with a six-pack of diet cola and several bags that looked like they might be people's lunches. She wished to look inside, but decided it was really none of her business and shut the fridge with a thump. She well knew that in every Staffroom kitchen there were wheels within wheels. People were quick to take offense about snooping into their lunches.

She smelled coffee from a plastic-lined garbage bin half-filled with empty cardboard coffee cups. She remembered suddenly that coffee nowadays cost as much as five dollars a cup! Stella wrinkled her nose.

Woolworths in Kerrisdale used to charge 35 cents for a cup of tea at the lunch counter. As an extra, you received a pleasant sense of elevation as you hoisted your behind onto the red naugahyde stool, where you could twist your seat back and forth while you waited for your tea. These days everywhere you went your teabag came in a little pack beside a cooling mug of water, and you'd have to fumble with the packet in a race to get the teabag into the water in time for something close to the hot drink you paid for. But thirty or forty years ago if you sat at the counter at Woolworths they brought your tea in a stainless steel teapot, the little square of paper flapping from its string out of the spout, like a tiny flag. The teapot handle burned your fingers at first, that was how beautifully hot it was, and you only poured half the tea into your squat, thick white cup—none of these enormous, hoggish cardboard cups—so that you could get them to pour more hot water on your bag. For 35 cents you could keep that one teabag on the go for an hour or more. She sighed. In the same way that the tea at Woolworths would be a little weaker as it got older and more used up, Stella felt a certain affinity with the teabag on its fourth go-round.

She chose a blue mug from among its less handsome brothers. Although she couldn't see a teapot, she had the basic building blocks for tea. She reached down a teabag from the box, noting with pleasure as she did so that even in this day and age the manufacturers of the tea still took the trouble to attach to each teabag by a little flag with a red rose on it. With the same sort of care, she set the teabag inside the blue mug and hung the little flag neatly on the outside rim.

Just as the kettle began to boil, Stella put her hand into her pocket. Something was inside. Money! She'd completely forgotten it was there. What was it? A five? A twenty?

She pulled out the thousand-dollar bill and stared

down at it.

First, she remembered why she had it.

Second, she decided that she might have made an error in taking it.

Third, and in a mad dash to be out of Fairmount's Staffroom before she was discovered, she made herself a cup of tea.

Not everybody her age would have enjoyed crouching down and sliding rear-end first under the folding art table in the storage room across the hall from the Staffroom, pulling a cup of tea along with her. But now that she had returned from forgetfulness to sanity she needed to think, and the table with its plastic-smelling cover gave her privacy—a blessed thing in this place of unlocked bedroom doors. Almost as blessed as this cup of tea.

What she needed to think about was this: How could she use this money to save Cheryl's job?

She sipped and contemplated the options available to her. Perhaps the best thing would be to tear it into bits and flush it down the toilet. Then the Director couldn't prove Cheryl had ever had it.

But, a thousand dollars! Down the toilet! Unthinkable.

Stella drained the last drops from the mug, and the tea bag bumped her lightly on the nose. She still had not decided what to do with the money in her pocket, but she felt a hundred times better. A thousand.

Maybe, instead of flushing the money, she ought to figure out who else could have stolen the other bills—eighteen of them.

Eighteen thousand dollars was a strange sort of number—a large amount of money, but not so much that you would consider yourself rich if you had it. Happy to get it, maybe, but not exactly rich.

Stella sucked her upper lip. Of course! There had to be more money than just eighteen thousand. She remembered the album she'd toed open in the Effects Cupboard, the album with Alice MacAndrew's photo in it. What had it been doing in there? Perhaps somebody had found the quiet closet and emptied the album of the bills hidden between the pages. There might be other albums, too, with even more money hidden inside…

She touched her tongue to the smooth rim of the mug and murmured to herself, "Whodunit, whodunit, whodunit…?" All the evidence pointed to Cheryl having taken all those bills from the coin album, but Cheryl was honest. So, who was not? Ollie, perhaps? He was so often around, and could hide anything in that sunny yellow trolley of his. Or Bellamy, Mrs MacAndrew's only relation and hope for continuation of the clan name? Or maybe the Director herself, Mrs Perdita Warren, who had searched the room for the antique coin and might easily have found the money? How terrible if the thief turned out to be any of these! Ideally, the perpetrator would be somebody from outside—a passing robber, who had spied through the window as the Dragon pawed her treasures, and awaited an opportunity to slip inside. It would be easy pickings—Alice MacAndrew was certain that she kept an unblinking eye on her family treasures, but she was in the washroom more often than her Swiss clock cuckooed.

With care not to dislodge the green plastic cover, Stella scooted carefully back out from underneath the table. She left the blue mug with its limp teabag behind in her secret hiding place as a sort of marker, the way astronauts left a flag on the moon. Then, fiddling thoughtfully with the bill in her pocket, she wandered down to the front entry to look out the window at the daffodils and think the case over.

She arrived just a moment too late. There before her, on the other side of the glass door, was a heart-rending sight. Cheryl, wearing her blue coat, was heading away from Fairmount Manor down the little walk with its striped awning, towards the driveway. In her arms she held a small box. Stella couldn't make out the individual contents, but the box seemed to be filled with bits and pieces, including a pot with a hyacinth that had not yet begun to bloom.

A nasty feeling took Stella by the shoulders. She had wondered whether she should have taken the money from Cheryl's pocket, and now she knew the answer. Or rather, she could see the outcome of her act.

Despite accusations of theft, it was obvious that Cheryl had not been fired. Dismissals, with their reviews and reports and paperwork, took weeks or longer. There had not been time to discharge the care worker. No, when the honest Cheryl had been unable to return the money Stella had stolen from her, Cheryl had quit.

This hurried departure was Stella's fault. Thus, it was up to Stella to put things right, and quickly too. Stella hauled on the door handle, but it didn't open—could not, without the door key. Stella ran to the reception kiosk and peered through the window at the desk, but the little room was empty of anybody who could open the door. She looked both ways along the corridor, but saw nobody. She might have run along the corridors, searching for Ollie or Reliza or any resident with key code status, but a glance at the front door told her that she was too late.

For here along the driveway came the next in the series of unhappy outcomes: Cheryl's husband driving that shining silver car. Cheryl's husband and children would be inside the car, perhaps wondering why on earth she wanted a ride home so early in her workday.

Stella ran back to the front door and pounded on the glass. When Cheryl didn't turn, Stella punched numbers into the key pad at random. But the door remained shut. Stella slumped against the glass, powerless to prevent the gleaming vehicle from pulling up in front of Cheryl. No sooner had the back car door slid open than Cheryl's three children, like small birds, fluttered out to alight about her. They attached themselves to her arms, to her legs. Children were weightless, Stella remembered. With their small bones and the lightness of their hope and love, you could pick them up as if they were made of feathers and set them on your hip. Cheryl did so now with the smallest of the three. This was a tousle-headed little girl...

Stella's arm, acting of itself, rose from her side and curved about the remembered shape of Junie's close embrace. "Shh," Stella whispered to her daughter down the long corridors of life. "Don't cry. We'll find a way to set things right." Stella found her own words of comfort impossible to believe.

Nor did Cheryl's spendthrift husband, meanwhile, appear happy with his wife's decision to leave her job. So abruptly did he hustle his offspring and then Cheryl herself into the car that Stella stared in disbelief. Did the husband not notice that when Cheryl climbed inside, her fingers were still resting on the top sill of the car door? Or might he deliberately have moved so quickly to slam it shut? Only an instant separated Cheryl from serious injury, but she'd released the door and her fingers were safe. Just in time.

But even a spendthrift could make a mistake slamming a car door. And even an idle man could truly love his wife.

Which only left a single question that Stella had to answer for the good of this little family, and for her own benefit as well.

How would it ever be possible to get Cheryl back to Fairmount Manor again?

CHAPTER ELEVEN

Her mind still stewing with self-recriminations, Stella entered Corridor Park. She gave little attention to occupants in the chairs along the walls, and so she paid the price.

Something caught her ankle. The hallway tilted like a cartoon spaceship. There followed a long drawn-out moment where all thought was dashed from her mind—all except a grim black-outlined notice reading *This is it! Your day to go out, Stella. And your final act in this world was to make Cheryl quit.*

But just as she reached the tipping point, from which no falling body can return, Stella felt a pair of arms come around her. A body pressed against her back and she and her salvation tottered there for a moment until the hallway righted itself and Stella, breathing hard, looked up into a pair of watery, but very blue eyes. Theo. Of all the male residents of Fairmount Manor, Theo Longbourne had the finest head of hair.

She looked up at him and said thank you. "I thought I was a goner," she admitted.

She became conscious that he was still holding her

by her forearms. Suddenly his hands began to tremble, and he let go.

"You're welcome," he said, and as far as she could recall, this was the first time he'd addressed a word to her directly. "Stella, I've always wanted to ask you…"

She never found out what he'd always wanted to know, because just then Theo stepped on her foot and apologized.

Stella was hardly conscious of his misstep. All she could think was that, for first time in a number of years, she'd been touched by a man who was not a medical professional. To her surprise, this moment recalled the old days, when she would be dancing with some fresh-faced, red-eared boy who trod on her toe. As a woman, it was up to her to take control of the situation. So, she looked up at him and said what a woman was meant to say: "You're very strong." And it was true. He might tremble, but he had caught her and had not let her fall.

From behind them, somebody laughed. Somebody on the far side of the corridor. Somebody with a wicked, dry laugh: Thelma Hu. Thelma was sitting a little way down from the three women Stella had for excellent reason dubbed the Greek Chorus, and it was Thelma's cane that had entangled itself with Stella's ankles. But Stella knew that was not why the blind woman was laughing at her.

Stella felt the colour rise in her cheeks. Across the corridor, the three members of the Greek Chorus looked up from their needlework. Iolanthe and Lucille eyed Stella with unblinking serenity, but she caught a truly poisonous stare from the Nodder.

"It's a sin how hard the linoleum is in this place." Iolanthe set her crewelwork down in her lap.

To Iolanthe's right, Lucille, the second member of

the Greek Chorus, jabbed a large needle in Stella's direction. "Fall on that floor, and it's murder."

"Murder by linoleum, in the first degree." Iolanthe looked pleased. Lucille held up her needle and thread, and the Nodder—the third and final member of the Greek Chorus—snipped off Iolanthe's thread with a small pair of scissors. "Just think how much easier it would be for the staff to run things if we all broke our necks."

"Some of us, certainly." Theo looked obliquely down at Stella, who trapped her lips between her teeth so as not to laugh out loud.

A tone sounded from the direction of the dining room. Iolanthe added, "Lunchtime. Something indigestible, as usual."

"Murder by cabbage," Lucille agreed, although the smell in the hall was clearly, recognizably, that of macaroni.

On Lucille's left, the Nodder nodded.

As if by a signal—and the tone that sounded lunch was, after all, just that—Theo turned away from Stella. He offered his arm to the Nodder. She looked up, and then rose, queen-like, to her feet. The Nodder took Theo's arm and they walked away towards the dining room, while Iolanthe and Lucille tidied their needlework into quilted bags and followed after them.

Stella found herself standing alone in Corridor Park.

Or rather, not quite alone. Behind her there remained the author of the mocking laugh. She heard the tap of metal on linoleum and turned to see blind Thelma Hu still in her seat. As Stella faced her, Thelma screwed up her face.

"If you're expecting me to say I'm sorry for tripping you, you're in for a long, cold afternoon's wait,"

Thelma said. She set one hand on the other atop the end of her cane, as if to stop Stella from taking it away from her.

CHAPTER TWELVE

"You tripped me on purpose, Thelma?" Not for the first time in proximity to Thelma Hu, Stella felt her temper expand against its seams. "And all this time I thought you didn't know what you were doing with that cane of yours."

Thelma, blind eyes hooded, shrugged. Above her head a poster featuring a dead branch on an arid landscape was stapled to the burlap-covered bulletin board. Lettered large upon the poster was the sentiment *Something lost brings something found. Something gained brings another loss.* This oppositional bit of nonsense on top of Thelma's laugh and shrug so irritated Stella that she turned her back to it and sat herself down in her usual chair next to Thelma.

"Thelma, I'm too old be falling on the linoleum. Watch where you put your cane."

"I would, but I'm blind," Thelma retorted. She turned her head sharply. "Who's that coming?"

Thelma's hearing must be acute. Stella hadn't heard a thing.

But now light, youthful footsteps sounded, and

here came Mrs Alice MacAndrew's granddaughter, arrived for her weekly visit with her aunt.

Young Bellamy was Mrs MacAndrew's only regular visitor. She advanced along the corridor, her good spirits supporting her in all the correct places. Her hair bouncing, her arms swinging... Bellamy was so young that Stella could no more resent her for it than she could begrudge a kitten its youth.

From her seat beside Thelma, Stella smiled at Bellamy. Bellamy smiled back. Stella heard a stealthy hiss of metal on linoleum. She reached out in time to grip Thelma's cane before she could trip the girl up.

With long, youthful strides, Bellamy walked by them, her large bag bumping against the back of her jacket. She would never know how close she'd come to taking a tumble.

Stella stared after her. That really was a very large handbag. A student's handbag, of a capacity to handle textbooks and maybe even a binder...

Or an album—coin album, photo album...

She said slowly, "Thelma, if an elderly person is being robbed of all her money, who is the first person you suspect?"

Thelma smacked her cane once against the floor. "Her accountant."

"I suppose so... But it would have to be somebody who was often inside her room here at Fairmount..."

"Don't beat around the bush," Thelma said. "I hear the rumours, just like everybody else. Are you asking whether Cheryl stole money from cranky old Alice MacAndrew?"

Cranky! Look who's talking! "But, if you leave Cheryl out?" Stella asked, "Who, then, is the most likely thief?"

Stella already knew the answer, but she didn't like it.

Thelma grunted. "You mean, the thief is not the trusted care worker? Well, then, it's a member of the family."

Stella sat quite still as Ollie came around the corner towards them. For such a large man, he moved quickly, like a great liner speeding across the Atlantic sea.

Stopping before them, Ollie said, "Better hit the chow line, ladies, before all that good nosh is gone."

"I'm not hungry," Thelma said.

"Now, Thelma, denial is a river in Africa." Ollie chuckled. "We all need to eat. Do you want me to help you down to the dining room?"

"What, do you think I'm blind?" Thelma grumbled.

"I'll go with her," Stella told him.

"That's the way, you pair of outlaws," Ollie laughed. Heading back towards the dining room, he called over his shoulder, "Unholster your six-shooters and hold up the chow wagon together."

Stella attempted to help Thelma to her feet, and got a bash from the cane for thanks.

"Of course it was the granddaughter who stole the money," Thelma said. "Young people don't have the same morality we do."

Stella frowned. She thought, but did not say aloud, That's just what a grouchy old girl like you would think.

"Same to you," Thelma said. "With knobs on."

"I didn't say that out loud." Stella shook her head as they walked along the corridor in the direction of the smell of wet pasta. "Did I?"

Thelma replied, "Ha! You'll never know."

CHAPTER THIRTEEN

Later that afternoon, while a nasty lunch of macaroni with grated egg was settling itself down for a long stay in her stomach, Stella sat in Corridor Park watching Bellamy, her visit to the Dragon apparently concluded, sashay past towards the foyer. Her enormous bag swung at her back below her long brown hair.

Stella made the clicking sound with her tongue that all teachers learned at teaching college.

If Cheryl hadn't stolen the money, then what were the chances that the Dragon's granddaughter Bellamy had? The problem was that jumping to conclusions such as the granddaughter stole the money was exactly what civilized legal systems were set up to avoid.

Furthermore, Stella liked Bellamy. While a careful observer might notice that her step dragged a little on the way to see the Dragon, and skipped when she left, the girl kept a pleasant face all the while. What was more, she never missed a visit. Stella appreciated that fact as only somebody with no visitors herself could.

Yet Occam's Razor and Agatha Christie's Miss Marple were in agreement. If the wife was murdered, look first at the husband. If the husband, watch the wife. When money is stolen, and there exists a young relative with a large handbag…

No. She would not judge the girl based on Thelma Hu's generalization.

She would, however, feel perfectly justified in proving her point. All she needed was a look inside Bellamy's capacious bag.

An idea was coming to Stella. But she would need help.

She murmured, "I need somebody to trip another person with her cane."

Thelma batted her cane against the leg of her chair. She said, "You've found your woman."

CHAPTER FOURTEEN

The fall that Stella had designed for Bellamy to take on her way back from her visit to her grandmother the following week was not a complete success. Or, rather, not at first.

Stella had expected that Bellamy would catch her ankle on Thelma's cane, lose her balance and try to save herself while her bag flew down the corridor. The idea was that the bag's contents would spread out along the floor in the sort of array in which brides used to lay out their wedding gifts for all to see. Instead, when Thelma tripped Bellamy, the girl went down flat while the handbag landed upright on the floor.

So erect did the bag stand, in fact, that Stella couldn't help taking its upright posture as a personal affront. Nothing at all fell out. The leather flap even stayed closed, almost as if daring somebody to look inside.

Meanwhile, the Greek Chorus watched the proceedings with interest.

"Are you all right, dear?" Iolanthe asked Bellamy gently. "Of course you are. Do young people have to be so noisy all the time?"

"They like to stir things up, that's what," Lucille answered. "Also, her skirt is too short."

The Nodder nodded.

Meanwhile, Bellamy was pulling herself into a sitting position on the floor. She looked up at Stella, confusion in her eyes.

"Are you hurt?" Stella asked.

"I'm okay."

"Good." Stella got to her feet. She took a deep breath. She picked up Bellamy's bag.

Then Stella tripped over Thelma's cane herself, just as Bellamy had, except that Bellamy hadn't done it on purpose. Stella's decision to trip herself was deliberate, but taken so swiftly that although she considered the consequences to the handbag, she overlooked the cost to herself.

Stella staggered forward. Her first action was to hold onto the bottom of Bellamy's handbag so that its contents flung themselves onto the corridor floor. She herself followed it down, almost in slow motion. Although it was not what you could truthfully call an accidental tumble, the anxious expression she knew she was wearing as she went down was perfectly honest.

On her knees now, Bellamy turned. She gasped, "Are you all right?"

"I… don't know." She truly did not. Despite the new agility she was feeling—the agility that dated from her morning exploration with Mad Cassandra—Stella had long been dreading a fall. She had thought any sort of full-body tumble might just finish her off, as a matter of fact, and had managed by taking extreme care to avoid wherever possible any uneven surface underfoot. Now, having taken such a fall on purpose (and it was a somewhat harder fall than she had planned on), she landed on the side of her hip with a feeling of doom. She checked her bones. She was astounded when they answered with a chipper, *All present and accounted for, sir.*

"I'm perfectly all right, thank you." Stella looked around her. The contents of Bellamy's bag had landed on the floor around Stella. A rosy makeup compact had slid as far along as the Greek Chorus's chairs, and lay underneath the Nodder's chair like some kind of small pink rodent running free in Fairmount Manor.

Stella peered at the bag's detritus splayed out across the floor: makeup, tissues, wallet, a sweater, a few books. Bellamy's phone had come to rest by Stella's right hand. As Bellamy folded her cardigan and tucked her makeup bag in her bag, Stella pulled the books towards herself. These needed checking out. She picked up each book by its cover. No thousand-dollar bills fell out.

Ha! Stella thought. Although she still had one item left to investigate, she already felt the pleasure of being right. Of course, Bellamy's innocence wouldn't help Cheryl get her job back, but Stella felt a sense of satisfaction about eliminating Bellamy as a suspect. And about being right that Bellamy was honest.

One final item should prove her case for the honesty of Youth. Bellamy's wallet—a small red leather affair—lay by Stella's knee. As a decoy, Stella slid the phone along the floor in Bellamy's direction. The girl bent down to scoop it up. Stella picked up the red wallet.

She was about to open it—to prove the girl's innocence—and look inside, when she saw a shadow fall across Bellamy's wallet. A long pair of tan-coloured trousers appeared in front of her. She looked up to meet Theo's gaze. His good hair fell over his forehead in a boyish manner, and in his eye she saw a question he was too polite to ask aloud: What are you doing with that girl's wallet?

But she had a query of her own, and hers was also internal: with Theo watching, how could she possibly peek inside the girl's wallet? For, if she was to be sure of the girl's innocence, she must do so.

She dropped her gaze and hoped Theo would move on. But he didn't budge from his spot, except to step out of Bellamy's way as she skated by them on her hands and knees, scooping up her belongings and replacing them in her bag.

Thelma's case against the girl could not be closed until Stella had checked the red wallet. She was beginning to think that Bellamy would never turn her back, and furthermore that she must by now have collected most of the contents of her bag. However, with a Sorry, excuse me! to the Greek Chorus, the girl was now peering under their chairs.

Now if Theo would just turn away to help Bellamy…

But Theo didn't move from his spot. He held out his hand.

Stella, heart sinking at the thought of having to figure out another way to finish her search, passed the wallet to Theo. As it travelled from her hand to his, a small miracle occurred. She felt the wallet open slightly. She leaned forward for a quick look before it could close again.

She saw, inside it, the last thing she wanted to see: the corner of something pink.

Damn.

As Theo handed the wallet to Bellamy, Stella used her chair to get herself back onto her feet. She sat back down beside Thelma and watched Theo escort the girl from Corridor Park towards her grandmother's room.

The Greek Chorus stirred and looked at one another.

"My, what a morning," Iolanthe said.

Lucille picked up her needlework. "That Stella! Pride goeth before a fall. But what about after the fall? That's what I want to know."

While the Nodder nodded, Thelma tapped her cane against the leg of Stella's chair. "Did it work?" she asked sotto voce.

"Yes. For my sins." Stella leaned back in her chair, feeling disappointed to her toes in Bellamy. And thoroughly annoyed that Thelma and the Greek Chorus had been right about the girl. "You were right. It was Bellamy who took the money. She is still taking it, apparently...and will continue to do so until Alice MacAndrew's stock of pink thousand dollar bills runs out."

"Ha," Thelma said. "I used to run a shop, you know. I know a thief when one walks into the room."

Now what? Stella shook her head. "Of course, there's nothing to be done about it. If I accuse Bellamy she will deny it. And denial..."

"...is a river in Africa. Don't try to fool me! What are you cooking up?" Thelma demanded.

"Nothing," Stella said tiredly. "I am out of ideas." But without even trying, she found that a new plan was forming in her mind. This one was more complicated than the last, darn it all.

Thelma moved her red silk slippers impatiently. She snapped, "Tell me."

What must it be like to be blind, sitting in Corridor Park every day of your life? Tapping your cane, waiting for a meal you hated the taste of? Stella sighed. "Actually," she began, "I hope to engage in a little... illegality..." As she explained the plan, it became clearer in her mind. And a little more unethical, too.

When she had finished, Stella thanked Thelma for listening.

"Don't thank me," Thelma retorted. "I'm listening for purely selfish reasons."

Stella nodded. "I feel the same way. The place is not the same without Cheryl."

"I don't care about Cheryl," Thelma snapped. "They'll hire another care worker in a second. What I like is that your plan is kinda interesting. It's the least bored I've been for several years."

Stella blinked. "Me, too."

CHAPTER FIFTEEN

Stella had to wait two full days for her opportunity—if you could call her days at Fairmount Manor full. Once she'd found an envelope for the money she'd taken from Cheryl—and once she'd found the perfect wording for the note on the outside of the envelope, the hours dragged. She spent them trying unsuccessfully to make small talk with Thelma, disliking the food served up by the Fairmount Manor cooks, reviewing her plans and trying not to drift away into some kind of grey-coloured reverie. In this way she awaited the Bellamy"s return to Daffodil Corridor. All that sustained Stella throughout the forty-eight hours was the knowledge that time was ticking away for Cheryl's job. For, with each hour that passed, her temporary replacement was settling deeper into her job.

As well, Stella had to remember that because of the tripping incident, one could no longer count on Bellamy taking her usual short-cut through Corridor Park to her grandmother's room. The girl might very well desire to give Thelma and her cane a wide berth. Therefore, in order not to miss any opportunity, Stella had to walk back and forth from Daffodil Corridor, through the office area, and around by the Activity Hall. These were all areas of Fairmount Manor where she often got lost among the many choices and turnings. Luckily, it didn't much matter whether she knew where she was going—the law of averages only suggested that she keep moving.

One embarrassing problem rose right away: as she walked about the place, she and Theo crossed paths now and then. Again, since Theo was famous for walking about Fairmount's corridors for most of the day, the law of averages compelled it. But after their second meeting in a matter of fifteen minutes, she began to worry that he would think she was some kind of stalker. Which she was, but Bellamy's stalker, not Theo's. After their third meeting, however, she greeted him with the same relaxed nod that he gave her.

So it was that two days later, her wandering paid off. She caught sight of the girl Bellamy as she entered the building. Stella had a sudden urge to call a fellow detective on a walkie-talkie with the news—Mad Cassandra, for choice. Instead, as Bellamy strode past Stella without sign of recognition, Stella silently broke from her previous trajectory. She tracked the girl past the stairwell and around the unnamed area leading to Daffodil Corridor, where Mrs MacAndrew's room faced Stella's.

She walked as quickly as her slip-ons would take her. Even so, she would never have caught Bellamy up except that the girl always did move comparatively slowly on her way in to see her grandmother. So, this part of the plan, the part where she followed the girl, was easy. As well, Stella had every right to be in Daffodil Corridor, where her own Room 34 was located, and thus must appear completely innocent of guile and subterfuge, which was lucky because Ollie might overhear her. The big care worker was busy with his yellow trolley not far from Alice

MacAndrew's door.

Stella inhaled deeply. She whispered to herself the count: "One... two... three..."

Now.

As she reached a point about twenty feet from Mrs. MacAndrew's door, Stella called out, "Bellamy, could you help me just for a minute?" She readied her prepared follow-up for the Sure thing, or Of course, that would follow.

But Bellamy turned and politely said, "I'm so sorry, but I'm late to see my grandmother, and she's always in such a mood. Excuse me...?"

As the girl headed for the Dragon's door, Stella scrambled for an opposing play. Before she could come up with a single idea, Ollie approached them and Bellamy gestured towards Stella and asked him, "Please, could you give this lady a hand?"

And then the girl ducked through the door into her grandmother's room.

Stella stared at the door as it closed pneumatically. She felt thwarted to her core.

Ollie said, "Sure, Stella, I'll give you a hand," and began to clap.

"Never mind, Ollie. Thank you," she said, trying to keep her annoyance under wraps. "I don't need any help after all."

"In that case, I think I'll take a little smoke break." He patted her shoulder and walked to the end of the corridor. Before disappearing through the fire door that led outside, Ollie flipped a switch too high up for most people to reach. He disappeared through it, patting his pockets in search of cigarettes or matches. The switch must have disarmed the door alarm, because it didn't sound. A crack of light down the length of the door showed that he had left it just fractionally open.

Alone now in the corridor, Stella examined the wreckage of her plan. How to resurrect it, when the girl would be gone in a flash once she'd seen her grandmother?

Without pleasure, Stella faced the fact that she would just have to summon the patience to wait a few more days until Bellamy visited again. And all the while, Cheryl's substitute care worker—Stella damned her as passable—was moving closer and closer to a permanent placement. Worse still, what if Cheryl took her Mona Lisa smile to another care home elsewhere in the city? No doubt that idle husband of hers would be itching for her paycheck.

No, if the thing were to be done, then best…Stella bit her lip, but supplied the all too obvious quote: "…it were done quickly."

She shuffled down to the end of the corridor by the fire door. There was a wall fire alarm there, the sort that was a red panel with a lever to pull that would break a glass rod and then sound an alarm throughout the building. She'd seen one of these set off before, at school. One afternoon a few decades back a student named Robbie Belkan, aged eight, had failed to take the elementary and vital precaution of checking over his shoulder and he had set off the fire alarm just as she was exiting the school library. So, Stella knew that the glass rod was not much of an obstacle to sounding the fire alarm. It was there just to let you know that should you pull the alarm, the stakes would be raised.

She pulled the red lever. The glass rod broke and dropped to the floor. Then all hell broke loose.

CHAPTER SIXTEEN

The noise was earsplitting. It even seemed to ratchet up during the first few seconds after she'd pulled the alarm. Taking a tip from young Robbie Belkan, she moved down the corridor, away from the fire door. Then she fell back against the wall, feeling jangled to the bones.

But the trouble—she thought she could safely call it that—had just begun. The corridor was filling now with residents heading towards the fire door. Walkers clattered, and residents chattered. Meanwhile, behind her, Ollie had banged the fire door open from the outside and was passing by with a distracted grin for Stella. He dived through Mrs MacAndrew's door. Of course Mrs MacAndrew, as the song went, would never walk alone, no further than her washroom anyway—not if it meant leaving the MacAndrew treasures behind. But Stella judged that the Dragon would find Ollie's help more than acceptable in a fire.

She was right. Here he came now, half-carrying the old woman. And here came Bellamy, following them. The girl appeared flustered, and was tucking her handbag over her shoulder.

Making haste, Stella stepped in front of Bellamy, cutting her off from her grandmother.

"Would you help me, dear?" Stella asked. "Please? Just let me take your arm…"

Said the spider to the fly.

"All right," Bellamy answered.

Stella caught hold of Bellamy's elbow.

"Walk a little slower, dear," Stella said, as residents made their way around them. The wheelchairs were passing now, along with the slower walkers, as they headed for the fire door here and, no doubt, at other designated fire exits around Fairmount Manor.

"But the fire…" Bellamy began.

"No worries about that," Stella assured her. "There is no fire. I pulled the alarm myself. I wanted to give you this envelope."

Stella took the envelope out of her pocket and handed it to Bellamy, who stared from it to her. Meanwhile, the parade of residents continued past the two of them.

Stella explained. "On the outside of the envelope is a note that you received from Cheryl several days ago, thanking your grandmother for her generosity but refusing it once she knew she'd been given real money. I wrote the note. Inside the envelope—no, don't open it—is a thousand dollar bill."

Bellamy opened her mouth to speak.

But Stella, conscious of the swift movement of time, pushed on, speaking clearly so as to be heard over the clanging of the alarm. "You know about the thousand dollar bills, of course—I saw one in your wallet the other day. They are quite a distinctive pink. I suppose you took the last one from the album…"

By now, Bellamy had come to a full stop in the

rapidly emptying corridor. She dropped Stella's arm and began, "I don't…"

Stella shook her head. "We don't have much time to work things out. Take the letter. I want Cheryl to come back. You don't want your grandmother to leave the rest of her wealth to the cat's home…"

Bellamy burst out, "I wish she would! Do you think that I want to spend my life looking after those things like she does?"

The alarm stopped short. Stella and the girl glared at each other in the sudden, oppressive silence.

Stella was even more disappointed in Bellamy after the girl's outburst. "I supposed you'd sell them once you'd inherited them."

"Of course I won't sell them." Bellamy looked ready to cry. "But I'm in first year university. I don't have any money…"

"That doesn't give you the right to…"

Now Bellamy was doing the interrupting. "Let me finish. I'm a MacAndrew. I know my duty. I'll keep the Chippendales and the Stubbs. I even love the prisms—I used to make rainbows with them when I was little. But I live in a student residence. You can't fit a quarter of the MacAndrew things in there, and they wouldn't be safe anyhow with everybody in and out all the time. I have to get a condo, but she'd never understand they don't give out houses for free just because you're a MacAndrew."

Light dawned. "You've been stealing a downpayment?" She recalled the photograph album she'd first found in the Effects closet, when all of this had begun. So, Bellamy had indeed snaffled more than one album full of money. "A downpayment for a place to live and store the MacAndrew treasures?"

"Of course. Do you think I'm a thief?"

Stella shot her a sharp look. "So you figured that the money would soon be yours anyway…? It's not, you know. But you're not the first person to bend the timeline for an inheritance. And now it's up to you to make things right." She took a breath. "Take the envelope. Give it to your grandmother. Be sure she straightens things out with the Director. Make sure you convince her that Cheryl is innocent."

"How?" Bellamy frowned. But she took the envelope.

Stella was running short on ideas. Still, one covert action should have been obvious to even the most reluctant and inexperienced thief. "For one thing, use the brain God gave you and move the other bits of money you haven't stolen yet around from the other albums so that your grandmother can be convinced she was mistaken about the theft of the other many thousands."

Bellamy slowed her pace. "Gosh, you're clever."

Stella sped up. "As for the Director, you'll think of a way. Use your youthful charm."

"But I don't…" The girl looked ready to cry.

Stella sighed. "Look, Bellamy, you made this mess, and I've done enough already. Take my arm and lead me out the front entry. We've been too long as it is, and I really am feeling quite tottery."

In silence the pair made their way through Corridor Park. As they neared the front door, Ollie, clearly on a mission to collect outstanding residents, spotted them. While he hurried towards them from the front door, Stella thought of one more thing.

She hissed, "Listen! Bellamy, you make sure your grandmother still thinks you love her."

Bellamy stared. She let go Stella's arm. Fiercely she said, "I do love her." Wiping eyes with her sleeve, she stalked away. She was a MacAndrew, all right.

As the girl passed him, Ollie took Stella's arm. He gave her an oblique, amused look. "Stella, best sella, you were standing near the alarm when it went off. Would you possibly know something about how that fire alarm happened to be pulled?"

Stella got a taste of how Bellamy must have felt a few minutes earlier. She decided that the young fire-alarm-puller Robbie Belkan had got it right: if caught, you had to play it cool. "How crazy do you think I am?" she asked primly.

"I don't think you're crazy," Ollie said. "I think you enjoy making things happen around this place. Don't worry. I won't tell."

"Thanks," Stella said, as he opened the door.

"Us outlaws got to stick together." Ollie laughed.

They stepped out under the awning to be checked off a master list only a few moments before the all clear sounded. To her disappointment, she got no more than a nose-full or two of spring air inside her before he led her back inside again.

CHAPTER SEVENTEEN

The following morning, Stella woke to the pleasant knowledge that she had solved the Bonnie Prince Charlie Mystery. The brouhaha was over and done with, as long as Bellamy made good on her promise to clear Cheryl's name. Two days later Stella knew for certain that this had been accomplished because Bellamy had stopped by to tell her so. The girl had been unable to meet Stella's eyes through much of the conversation, but Stella was satisfied that everything was cleared up regarding Cheryl's honesty with Bellamy's dragonish grandmother as well as with Mrs Warren, the Director of Fairmount Manor.

But if everything was really going to be all right, then why was there such a heavy feeling in the air? Something was still wrong. Three days after Bellamy had cleared Cheryl's name with the Warden, the care worker was still not back at Fairmount Manor. Stella shook her head. She left Room 34 and walked down Daffodil Corridor. With every step her uneasy feeling grew stronger.

So it was that as she made her way past the Staffroom, she was unsurprised to see Reliza standing hunched over in the middle of the room, wiping her eyes with the bottom hem of her yellow nylon smock. As ever, Stella wished Reliza would get something new for herself.

Stella looked both ways. Then she stepped out of the corridor, where she was supposed to be, and into the Staffroom, where she was not. Guiltily she remembered making a cup of tea in here.

Reliza looked up as Stella entered the room. "Oh, Stella…." Her expression was tragic. "I said all along that Cheryl wouldn't steal."

"You did say that," Stella agreed. "And so did I… Now, when is Cheryl coming back?"

Reliza's eyes filled again. "It's so unfair." Her face turned pink, so that she looked prettier than ever, despite that old yellow smock. "They wouldn't treat a doctor so, or even a nurse. Just us care workers…"

Stella nodded. She had been hearing that complaint most of her life: Unfair! When you spent your life teaching in an elementary school, you heard it almost every day. It's not fair, Mrs Ryman, the whole class has to stay in because of one spitball. It's so unfair, Stella, the administration took my Grade Two class and gave it to the new teacher.

But she tried to think of a single decision handed down in school, in life or even in the law that was fair for everybody—not impartial, but fair, so that all parties were content with the outcome. Stella could not. Decisions everywhere were met with generous acceptance, guilty greed, victorious joy, silent resignation—but never happiness all around. In fact, if Cheryl finally did get her job back, the new girl they'd brought in to take her place, who had her own living to make, would lose out…

As Stella contemplated fairness, Reliza sat down at the Staffroom table. Stella watched her do it. The young care worker didn't set her hands on the table to ease the sitting down the way Stella did, and nothing went crack when Reliza bent her knees. Nor did she let out a deep breath to mark the end of the sitting procedure. With youthful ease, Reliza simply sat. Behind her, the sun shone through the window and struck lights from the girl's dark hair. No, the world was not fair.

Stella said, "You ought to talk to the Director. Make her see that Cheryl must be rehired."

Reliza's hands were shaking. "I would like to. I would. But, Stella, what if Mrs Warren takes against me? She could find a way to fire, me, too. And without a job, how do I stay in the country?"

"Cheryl wasn't fired, she quit, Reliza. And your union…" Stella began, but trailed off, sensing the futility of this line of argument with this particular young woman.

Just then a rattle of buckets and wheels sounded outside the Staffroom door, and Ollie stepped inside the Staffroom. As he made his way to the sink she noticed, as always, how lightly he moved for such a big man.

He took a mug down from the cupboard over the sink and gave Stella a quizzical look.

Stella grimaced. "Of course, I know that a Staffroom is meant to be private, but…"

Ollie interrupted. "Oh, what the hell! It's good for you and it doesn't hurt us, does it, Reliza? It's nice to have company in here now and then…"

He paused as Reliza buried her face in her hands.

Stella turned to Ollie. "Cheryl didn't steal anything. It's been proven."

I proved it, she thought, first with satisfaction and then with an expanding resentment at the unchanged outcome of the case. She'd set out to prove Cheryl innocent so that the poor woman, wracked with debt and up to her ears in young children and a spendthrift husband, would be rehired. And Cheryl was not rehired.

Stella stared fiercely past Ollie at the row of coat hooks at the back of the Staffroom near the washroom, where Cheryl's blue trench coat ought to be hanging right now. It had been quite a struggle, proving Cheryl innocent. And struggles have nothing to do with fairness. They are about getting what you struggle for: the reward at the end of the fray.

So, it came down to this.
1. Stella had won.
2. Therefore, she should get Cheryl back as her favourite care worker.

"I tell you what," Stella said. "I'm going to see the Director about this myself."

Ollie chuckled. "You go, Stella my bella," he said.

Stella looked sharply at him. Ollie was jovial, apparently by nature as well as physiology. And joviality was only a hop skip and jump from making fun of a person.

Ollie raised his mug of water to her. "Stella to the rescue," he said.

Was he making fun?

She decided that she didn't care. She turned her back on the two care workers—Reliza, so loving and absolutely no help whatsoever, and Ollie, happy with things as they were. Stella headed down the corridor towards the Office.

Often, over the months since she'd moved to Fairmount Manor, Stella had been critical of the rambling nature of the institution's design. It seemed to her that an eight-year-old with a ruler and a box of crayons could have planned a more sensible route of corridors for the convenience of residents and staff. The layout was particularly distressing if you were the sort of person who, like Stella, often found yourself standing halfway along a corridor, uncertain which was the way to your own room, and feeling like a child lost in Sears. But just now she was glad it was a long way to the office, because she had to think what exactly she was going to say to the Director of Fairmount Manor.

All along the way, however, she could think about nothing except the shuffling sounds her slip-on shoes made on the corridor linoleum, and how the air was even heavier than it had been earlier. She filled her lungs with it and nodded to herself. No wonder. Lunchtime loomed, and with it something involving cooked celery.

By the time she reached the office, she had developed no plan at all. Less certain of herself now than when she had set out from the Staffroom, she rested for a moment in front of the Director's secretary's empty desk.

How many weeks had it been since the Director's secretary had retired at the end of what Stella believed must have been a long and gratingly efficient career? For whatever reason, the secretary had not been replaced. Perhaps it was a budget issue—or maybe somebody had finally invented a phone system that did filing.

But it meant that nobody barred the way to the Director's door. And the door stood ajar. In the circumstances, there was only one thing to do. Soldier on, Stella.

Pulling her back as straight as she could make it, Stella walked inside Mrs Perdita Warren's private office. Without knocking. Stella was certain that, even if nothing and nobody else was behind her, surprise was on her side.

The office was empty. That was fine. Metaphorically speaking, Stella would lie in wait.

CHAPTER EIGHTEEN

Where was she? Stella closed her eyes, trying to get a sense of place. After an unsuccessful moment, she opened them again. Gazing from wall to door to window to wall, she gained a sense of… office.

Her own office? She'd always had a small office of her own, behind the school library circulation desk. This office didn't look like hers, but from time to time she would return from the summer holidays to find that workmen from the School Board had redecorated her space. She didn't think much of these colours—she preferred a warm white to this spleen-like deep apricot. But if she were to tack book jackets up on the walls, they would hide the worst of it.

And, my goodness! Stella thought, folding her hands on the desk before her. This was the first time they had given her a new desk! It was a little too large for the space, mind you. And somebody had done a job on her usually tidy stacks of class lists and titles to reorder. These were strewn around and even had coffee mug rings on them. She supposed the custodians must have been watching hockey games in here again, courtesy of the school cable television. Ah, well.

She listened for the morning bell, and for the rising rhubarb of students' voices out in the hall that meant it was almost time for class to begin.

But there was nothing. All was quiet. Was it after school, then? A foolish question, Stella! As if she didn't know the time…

She would take a few moments to straighten her desk.

Sliding backwards on her rollered chair, Stella opened the top drawer. She touched the contents. "These are not mine," she said, irritated with the custodians, who must have switched the drawers without checking them. "I have never seen these things in my life."

A shadow fell across the desk, and Stella looked up into the face of a woman she knew only slightly. For the moment, she couldn't recall the woman's name.

But the woman knew hers. "Stella, please close that drawer and come around to this side of my desk."

My desk? Stella was taken aback, but her eye fell on a black nameplate lying knocked over among the papers. If this was her desk, it ought to read Mrs S. Ryman. She did her best to focus on it, but the letters shifted and interwove alarmingly. Summoning just that touch of dignity that had always seen her through the type of embarrassing situations that couldn't be shrugged off by laughing at herself, she touched the nameplate and looked up at the other woman. "Is this you?"

The woman sighed. "That's right. I am Mrs Perdita Warren, Stella. I am the Director of Fairmount Manor."

Stella nodded. "Glad to meet you, Perdita."

There followed that sort of pause that tells you something is amiss.

At last the director said, not unkindly, "I'd be more

comfortable if you called me Mrs Warren."

Oh, my, Stella thought with a rush of relief. Now we know where we are. Fairmount Manor bloomed up around her. "Of course," she said, rising. "And I, too, would prefer to be called Mrs Ryman."

"As you like." Mrs Warren frowned. "It's up to you to make your preferences known, Mrs Ryman."

With gentle hands the Director propelled Stella out from behind the desk. Mrs Warren added, "We're not mind readers, you know."

With a desk drawer full of things like that, you must be getting close, Stella wished to say. Manners, plus a sense of walking a fine invisible line, prevented her from doing so.

The Director followed Stella's gaze and snapped the drawer shut on at least a dozen—perhaps more— puzzle magazines. Sudoku, Anagrams, Crosswords. Cryptic crosswords! The woman must be sharp as one of Iolanthe's needles.

Stella turned to leave the office. She was in the doorway when the sight of the empty receptionist's desk recalled her errand to her at last. Cheryl needed Stella's support if she was to return to Fairmount Manor.

So close had she come to forgetting what she was there to do that it was almost like having the great glowing finger of God write her a reminder note on the wall: *Stella, be not vague.* Be compos. Be sharp! Stella turned and shuffled back across the office to the Director's desk. There, she waited a long moment and then another, longer still.

At last, Mrs Warren looked up. "Do you want help finding your way, Stella?"

Stella pinned her with a look.

The Director corrected herself. "...Mrs Ryman?"

"Mrs Warren, I would like to know how soon we may expect to see Cheryl back working among us?"

Mrs Warren took a moment, apparently deciding how—and, perhaps, whether—to answer her. "I can't say, not at this point in time. Her replacement has been quite satisfactory, I think you'll agree…"

Anger washed through Stella. She forced herself to show only calm. "Her substitute," Stella corrected her.

Mrs Warren wrote a few words on the top sheet of paper. She frowned at them. Then erased them and moved the top sheet to the bottom.

Soldier on.

Stella continued, "Of course, I'm thinking of the union base and the trouble it may bring you."

Mrs Warren looked up sharply. "Union base? What do you mean?"

Ah. Stella shook her head. "I worked for decades in a school system, not in a care home like Fairmount Manor, but these union bases are all the same, I believe? All they have to do to cause trouble for you is to spread about a story regarding Cheryl quitting because of mental torment due to unfounded charges of theft…"

"But…" Mrs Warren began.

Stella ploughed a straight line through the interruption. "… a story of a single mother recently abandoned by her husband. A mother of two young children. And on top of that, they will produce her unblemished record of selfless service, followed by unjust accusations… the union is just like a dog with a bone! And of course, they're all in tight with the left-wing press, aren't they?"

Mrs Warren sat back in her chair. She gazed at Stella without expression. She said nothing.

Stella's instinct told her to carry on.

"What my school district would do in such a case," Stella went on, "was to put together a little package…"

Here instinct instructed Stella to pause a moment, so she did. She was a teacher and a school librarian. She knew how to wait, that was certain.

At last Mrs Warren asked, "What kind of package do you mean, Mrs Ryman?"

Stella inclined her head. "It would include a card of appreciation." Beyond perusing the bimonthly teachers' union newspaper, Stella's knowledge of the inner workings of management and unions was limited, and she was inventing freely now. "And certainly a raise—smallish, if it came early. Uncomfortably large, if the union people became involved. Well, it's something to think about, when you make that call to Cheryl."

Mrs Warren glanced at the phone.

Stella added, "…before you get a phone call yourself. From the union, the press…" She thought hard. "…and your Board of Directors. How nice to be able to say it's all handled."

Mrs Warren blinked.

Stella said, "And it would be a good thing to spread the news of Cheryl's return around the staff, as well, wouldn't you say? Put a stop to any unrest?"

Mrs Warren stood. "I'll show you out, Mrs Ryman."

But Stella was on a roll. Great things were in the air, and something more was needed. It was rather like the time she'd taken over the school Spring Concert from a faltering administrator. She said, "And by the way, could you please write down for me the number code for the front door? I'm feeling much better these days, as you see. I would like to be able to take myself outside for a walk from time to time."

Mrs Warren frowned.

One thing Stella knew, in negotiations the impetus of gain must not be lost. "I know that when I was brought here..." Stella could not remember who had brought her in to Fairmount Manor—A doctor? A neighbour? —so she hurried past that part. "...I was not myself. I was ill, you know, with all the difficulties in orientation that illness brings..." Here, a chuckle. "... to an old lady. But, I'm feeling quite myself, now..."

She trailed off.

Mrs Warren was shaking her head. She said, "Mrs Ryman, five minutes ago you were sitting at my desk as if you believed it to be your own."

Stella thought hard, but before she could come up with any sort of reasonable reply, Mrs Warren went on.

"And, Mrs Ryman, you checked yourself in. You begged to be admitted, as a matter of fact. Let me tell you, Mrs Ryman, exactly what you told me.

"Let us start with the incident where you set your house on fire."

Stella's only thought made a circle in her mind: Oh.

CHAPTER NINETEEN

Burning with embarrassment and shame at learning what state she'd been in upon her arrival here at Fairmount, Stella shuffled along the hallway towards Corridor Park. She tried not to think about the things Mrs Warren had told her—how Stella had left a box of tissues on her kitchen stovetop to burst into flame, and how she had wept while she pled with Mrs Warren for admittance to Fairmount Manor.

Stella rounded the corner into Corridor Park. In the row of chairs to her left, the Greek Chorus sewed as hard as Odysseus's wife Penelope in the daylight hours, before she ripped her tapestry to pieces at night in order to avoid remarrying. Smart girl, that Penelope. Smarter than Stella with her former lodger, all those years ago.

Stella grimaced. There was another thing she hated to think about: her long-ago lodger.

Iolanthe looked up from her fancywork. "Stella, dear, you make everybody nervous, running around like a teenager all the time."

"Sit down and give us all a rest," Lucille added.

The Nodder nodded. She pulled her small scissors

from the pocket of her fleece vest and snipped Iolanthe's threads for her.

"Won't you sit down with us?" Iolanthe said, and nobody could have phrased the invitation more pleasantly than she. Her face was pleasant and her tone was sweet, so why was it that every time Iolanthe addressed her, Stella always felt she'd been pinged in the behind by Iolanthe's crewelwork needle?

"No, thank you." She walked by the Greek Chorus. She thought about walking on, out of Corridor Park, never to return. But what then? The Activities Hall? Bridge foursomes? Healthy Movement? Never. So it was this, or her room.

She sat herself down in her own chair under the skylight. Beside her Thelma slumped, as she so often did, with the tip of her cane between her Chinese silk slippers, her feet flat on the floor.

Stella asked, "Do you mind if I invade your privacy?" She meant to sound jokey and even friendly, but the words hung in the air between her chair and Thelma's.

"Why should I mind?" Thelma asked. "You smell all right, so far."

Stella rolled her eyes and tried not to laugh out loud. Needles darting away on one side of the corridor, personal remarks on the other. Stella sighed as Thelma's cane moved over and somehow got in a tangle with Stella's ankles. Stella got the cane sorted out just as the tone sounded for dinner.

The dinner tone! Stella had come to understand that it signaled the Nodder's great moment of the day. For now, round the corner closest to Iolanthe and farthest from Stella he walked: Theo, with his upright posture and excellent hair. He was wearing a sweater in a shade of pale lemon that told Stella that a woman had picked it out for him. Knowing how women shopped, she thought he probably owned a second one as well, of identical styling but in sky blue or mint green. The yellow suited him, though.

As Theo walked slowly towards Greek Chorus, the Nodder tucked her little scissors into her pocket and sat up in a posture of calm anticipation. Stella nodded to herself.

Dignity. Consideration. Theo represented both these virtues in a place where Stella was not even allowed to bathe herself without supervision.

In a moment he would offer the Nodder his arm and take her down to lunch.

That lemon yellow sweater of his brought to mind her high school years, and a clique of handsome boys from the rugby team who wore shirts and sweaters in Easter Egg tones—aqua and lemon, mint green and sky blue. She had liked the look of the boy who wore aqua. She couldn't recall his name, but she did remember the way he walked right past her in the school corridor, heading for another girl, just as Theo was approaching the Nodder now.

And that was fine with Stella. There came a time when you no longer cared whether you were the chosen girl, and maybe that was how you knew you had grown up to be a self-sufficient woman. Or maybe not. Maybe you just got used to not being chosen and convinced yourself, through steady repetition, that you didn't care.

Stella didn't care. At eighty-two she was so evolved that she would once again simply admire the composure with which Theo offered the Nodder his arm. And although it was impossible to like the Nodder, Stella always got a kick from the pleasure with which the Nodder took Theo's arm. It might well be the closest that the woman got to happiness these days. Stella had to admit, despite her aversion to the Nodder, that she appreciated the modest way in which the Nodder cast down her gaze each time she accepted Theo's arm. And every time she watched the exchange of courtesies, Stella liked Theo a little bit more.

Iolanthe and Lucille tucked their sewing away under their seats. The Nodder sat up straight and ready.

"I'm blind, you know," Thelma muttered. "You'd think that once he'd offer to take me to dinner."

"Ollie or another care worker always comes by for you," Stella said. She shifted uncomfortably. "But I'll take you to dinner if you like."

"Don't bother yourself," Thelma answered, batting about with her cane and catching Stella between the ankles.

But, now Theo walked past the Greek Chorus—past the Nodder! —and stopped in front of Stella. She looked up into his watery blue gaze and felt suddenly foolish and very elderly.

Theo offered Stella his arm.

"No, really," Stella said awkwardly. "I'm perfectly all right."

As if she hadn't spoken, he stood, gazing down at her. His calm told her that he had all the time in the world. Stella hesitated, untangled herself from Thelma's cane and stood. She took his arm. Together they walked towards the far end of Corridor Park.

But before they'd taken five steps in the direction of the dining room, it seemed to Stella that a black cloud was descending from the ceiling. It drifted along the corridor and settled over the Nodder.

Stella gave a mental shrug. She was enjoying the feel of her arm looped through Theo's. The Nodder, for once, could do without—the experience might even improve her.

Stella looked up at Theo. "This is very kind of you," she said.

Theo didn't answer. They shuffled down few steps further along the corridor. But, along with the pleasant, almost-forgotten sensation of receiving special attention from the most attractive man around, no matter how taciturn and watery-eyed, Stella felt a sudden spiritual discomfort.

She tried to ignore it, but Guilt will have its little say.

Shut up, she told Guilt. Still, she couldn't help looking back along Corridor Park between the next two steps. The Nodder's gaze met hers, and Stella was reminded again of the girl she'd been in high school, standing with her back against her locker, watching the boy in the aqua cardigan go by, holding a prettier girl's hand.

She looked back again. The Nodder stared after them, her eyes dark in her closed-up face.

Am I a high school girl? Stella wondered. Or, more realistically, is there still a high school girl inside me somewhere?

Placing her free hand on his lemon-coloured sleeve, Stella stopped Theo before they rounded the corner.

"You have to go back for her, Theo…"

When he looped her arm back through his, Stella turned them both around. She led him all the way back into Corridor Park. There, she handed him over to the Nodder.

The two of them walked off. Stella sat down suddenly. Such an expenditure of goodwill had exhausted her.

"I guess you think you're some kind of hero now," Thelma said, tapping her cane on the floor.

Stella sat down beside her. "I don't know why I keep thinking you're blind, Thelma."

"Would they make me carry this damned cane everywhere I go if I wasn't?"

Stella's stomach rumbled. She and Thelma were alone in the corridor now, and the smell of wet pasta drifted down upon them from the dining room. Somebody must have gotten a deal on fusilli, Stella thought. This was the second day in a row. Or maybe the third.

"The Chinese invented pasta," Stella said. "I think it came to Europe via Venice."

Thelma said, "We should have left well enough alone."

One beat later, Stella said, "If anybody ever listened to us, they would think we're just a couple of old grouches."

"Everybody's grouchy at Fairmount Manor," Thelma said. "Tell whoever's listening, you'd be cranky, too."

"We're all cranky because nothing ever changes," Stella said. But this statement turned out to be untrue. For, once on her feet, she astonished herself by offering her arm to Thelma.

And, flabbergastingly, Thelma took it. Together, the two women shuffled and clattered out of Corridor Park. They were already late for lunch.

END

Looking for more mysteries to devour?

Don't miss the
Stella Ryman Fairmount Manor Mysteries series
by this author.

More Stella Novellas and Novelettes:

#1, Stella Ryman and the Fairmount Manor Mysteries

#2, The Poison Pen Affair

#3, The Four Digit Puzzle

#4, The Case of the Vanishing Resident

#5, Stella and the Thief Named Edge

#6, Stella Ryman and the Man with the Gun

#7, The Death of a Crusader

#8, The Ghost at the End of the Bed

#9, The Mystery of the Mah-jongg Box

And more to come…

Next in the
Fairmount Manor Mysteries,
Stella Novella #2,
"The Poison Pen Affair"
By Mel Anastasiou

Mrs Stella Ryman is
an amateur sleuth,
trapped in a down-at-heel care home.

Stella Ryman.
You'd be cranky too.

Malice and danger mount as a series of letters are delivered by mysterious means to staff and residents in Fairmount Manor. In this second Stella Novella, things get very personal indeed.

Excerpt from

Stella Ryman and The Poison Pen Affair

Stella Novella #2

Mel Anastasiou

CHAPTER ONE

A whisper of sound woke Stella. Or did not exactly awaken her, but made her aware that she was awake. She felt a frisson between her shoulders and an inexplicable sense that something was approaching her room. "I'm getting up," she told her mother, who had died so long ago. Stella pictured her leaning out at the gold bar of heaven. Stella's mother held three lilies in her hand, and she was saying, *Stella, stir the porridge*.

Stella shook herself. Imaginings like that one in a younger woman might feel poetic, but at eighty-two they sounded cuckoo. Therefore Stella employed Holmesian investigative techniques to impose order on her early morning thought processes. The scope for investigation inside her little institutional bedroom was narrow, but in Fairmount Manor, a person used what she had or used nothing. So, lying quite still with her eyes shut tight, Stella strained to hear whether the whispering sound would come again.

What was that? Just the quack of a weighted door shutting itself somewhere in Daffodil Corridor.

And now, the mewing of Ollie's trolley's wheels nearing and then passing by Stella's room.

But, the strange little noise that had wakened Stella in the first place had sounded more like a snake's hiss, although snakes were obviously unlikely early callers in Fairmount Manor. The whisper didn't come again, but nobody—not even Mrs Perdita Warren, the Director of Fairmount Manor, with all her administrative powers— could stop Stella enjoying this small mystery.

She opened her eyes and looked about her. Room 34 had not been built to please, but early sunshine shone through the window over her bed. She dipped her hand into the square patch of sunlight that warmed her belly and turned her nightgown from white to soft yellow. From the laminate bedside table that Fairmount Manor provided for residents she took her glasses from atop the soft red cover of *The Prisoner of Zenda*. This was the book that Cassandra had given her in the Effects Closet a few days earlier, just before locking Stella inside. Stella was enjoying rereading this elderly copy of *Zenda*, as much for its thick, cotton-y pages as for the rip snorting story it told.

She set her glasses onto her nose. And that was when she saw it: a white rectangle on the gray linoleum floor. The intriguing whisper of sound had heralded its delivery into her room, under her door.

Somebody's written me a letter. Her heart began to beat too quickly for health. An unwelcome image muscled its way to the front of her mind: it was the memory of just such a letter—a single envelope, unstamped, which had arrived at her home a few months before she'd come to Fairmount Manor. And the thought of that earlier envelope, lying on the front door mat of the house she'd sold to come to Fairmount, made Stella feel sick to her stomach.

She touched her palms to her cheeks—the sort of touch that her mother always used to calm Stella down in a childhood crisis. *They never leave us, do they? One's parents, I mean.* She thought of her own daughter, Junie, and wondered whether it was the same for her, despite everything. Did her daughter ever wake to feel Stella's arms around her and her cheek against hers?

The envelope lay with one corner hidden under the bottom edge of the door.

She stared at the letter. *Don't be afraid.* But she was afraid--fearful that somehow her name would be written on the envelope in strong, masculine, backward-slanting letters. *Mrs Stella Ryman,* standing out clearly in green ink.

Her breath stopped. She was right to feel afraid. He'd found her.

"No, he has *not,*" Stella said aloud. "Once a fool, always a fool, Stella Ryman. That man is far away. This is only a letter somebody else has sent you."

But who? No other letter had arrived under her door since her arrival at Fairmount. She threw aside her slippery duvet and prepared to address the question.

Through long habit she rolled, knees first, towards the edge of the bed furthest from the wall. This movement took her through that bitterly painful angle that she could never seem to avoid when sitting up, no matter which part of her she led with. Once her feet were on the floor she stood up carefully, being long past the age where she found stretching an unmixed pleasure. She walked to the door and gazed down at the envelope. She turned it round with a bare toe and read her name in bold print.

Just as she was about to bend down to pick up the envelope, she realized who must have sent it. Fairmount's Director, Mrs Perdita Warren, must have shoved it under Stella's door to be opened and read smartly upon rising. Stella gave a sniff and turned away. As far as she was concerned, any written directives from that woman could languish on the linoleum tile until it, or the linoleum, rotted. Back ramrod stiff, Stella washed her face at the sink in her little washroom and pulled on her fleece jacket and trousers over her underclothes. But as she was folding her nightgown under her pillow, she wondered whether her deduction had been correct. There had been something about that letter that didn't jibe with an administrative epistle.

Stella approached the envelope with renewed interest. One hand on the door for balance, she picked it up and straightened again. The envelope was a little longer than it was wide, her name printed boldly upon it. With some surprise she observed that her name on the white envelope was not typed or handwritten, but *assembled.* The black and white letters appeared to have been cut out, likely from a magazine, and glued onto the envelope. She slid her glasses a little farther up on her nose.

She had never seen the like, outside of police dramas on television. The cut-out letters gave the missive the air of a ransom note. She ran her thumb over the letters, and found that the glue—or rather white paste—was still slightly tacky around the perimeter of her name.

That was interesting. So, the letters had been glued on so recently that they were not quite dry. Stella turned the envelope over. She noted that it was the sort of envelope that Christmas cards came with, the kind that had glue only at the bottom edge and not the sides, so that you could slip your thumb under the flap and open it quite easily. She remembered always having extra envelopes of this sort around, extras from Christmas cards she'd made errors on and had ripped up and tossed out. As she ran her thumb along the flap, she wondered whether she'd send out Christmas cards this year. But whom did she want to trust with the information that she had sold her house and moved into a care home?

Stella slipped her thumb under the flap.

Somebody knocked at the door. Stella started. Some instinct for secrecy caused her to slip the envelope out of sight between the thick pages of *The Prisoner of Zenda*. Straightening the hem of her zip jacket, and feeling a little foolish, she turned to answer the door.

Look for **Stella Ryman and The Poison Pen Affair** for sale September 2014.

Thank you very much indeed for your interest.
Stella and I appreciate all the kind reviews we receive more
than we can ever say. All good things to you always.

Mel Anastasiou

Printed in Great Britain
by Amazon.co.uk, Ltd.,
Marston Gate.